Samuel French Acting Edition

I0591848

A Taste of Things to Come

by Debra Barsha
& Hollye Levin

SAMUELFRENCH.COM   SAMUELFRENCH.CO.UK

FOR PRODUCTION ENQUIRIES

UNITED STATES AND CANADA
Info@SamuelFrench.com
1-866-598-8449

UNITED KINGDOM AND EUROPE
Plays@SamuelFrench.co.uk
020-7255-4302

Each title is subject to availability from Samuel French, depending upon country of performance. Please be aware that *A TASTE OF THINGS TO COME* may not be licensed by Samuel French in your territory. Professional and amateur producers should contact the nearest Samuel French office or licensing partner to verify availability.

MUSIC USE NOTE

Licensees are solely responsible for obtaining formal written permission from copyright owners to use copyrighted music in the performance of this play and are strongly cautioned to do so. If no such permission is obtained by the licensee, then the licensee must use only original music that the licensee owns and controls. Licensees are solely responsible and liable for all music clearances and shall indemnify the copyright owners of the play(s) and their licensing agent, Samuel French, against any costs, expenses, losses and liabilities arising from the use of music by licensees. Please contact the appropriate music licensing authority in your territory for the rights to any incidental music.

IMPORTANT BILLING AND CREDIT REQUIREMENTS

If you have obtained performance rights to this title, please refer to your licensing agreement for important billing and credit requirements.

A TASTE OF THINGS TO COME was produced by Bucks County Playhouse (Producers: Alexandra Fraser, Robyn Goodman, Stephen Kocis, and Josh Fiedler; in association with Staci Levine) on February 2, 2016. The production was directed and choreographed by Lorin Latarro, with music direction by Lena Gabrielle, scenic design by Steven C. Kemp, costume design by Dana Burkart, lighting design by Nathan W. Scheuer, projection design by Stephen Stivo Arnoczy, and sound design by Matthew Given. The production stage manager was Veronica Aglow. The cast was as follows:

JOAN SMITH	Ariana Shore
CONNIE OLSEN	Erin Mackey
AGNES CROOKSHANK	Gina Naomi Baez
DOTTIE O'FARRELL	Allison Guinn

A TASTE OF THINGS TO COME received its Off-Broadway premiere, produced by York Theatre Company (James Morgan, Producing Artistic Director; in association with Staci Levine), on November 17, 2016. The production was directed and choreographed by Lorin Latarro, with music direction by Gillian Berkowitz, scenic design by Steven C. Kemp, costume design by Dana Burkart, lighting design by Nathan W. Scheuer, sound design by Daniel J. Gerhard, props design by Kate Stack, and projections design by Justin West. The production stage manager was Veronica Aglow. The cast was as follows:

JOAN SMITH	Paige Faure
CONNIE OLSEN	Autumn Hurlbert
AGNES CROOKSHANK	Janet Dacal
DOTTIE O'FARRELL	Allison Guinn

A TASTE OF THINGS TO COME received its Chicago premiere, produced by Staci Levine, at the Broadway Playhouse on March 20, 2018. The production was directed and choreographed by Lorin Latarro, with music direction by Kara Kesselring, scenic design by Steven C. Kemp, costume design by Dana Burkart, lighting and projection design by Nathan W. Scheuer, and sound design by Daniel J. Gerhard. The production stage manager was Hollace Jeffords, and the general manager was 321 Theatrical Management. The cast was as follows:

JOAN SMITH	Cortney Wolfson
CONNIE OLSEN	Libby Servais
AGNES CROOKSHANK	Linedy Genao
DOTTIE O'FARRELL	Marissa Rosen

CHARACTERS

JOAN SMITH – Twenty-four, married for six years. Her husband, Bob, is a traveling salesman. Her real name: Chaia Bayla Frankel. Born to Jewish immigrant parents who changed their name upon arriving at Ellis Island right before the start of WWII. She has not told anyone that she's Jewish. The other girls are slightly jealous of her because she appears to "have everything." She smokes. Hairdo: Annette Funicello. Fashion sense: 1950s sophisticated (Act One), hippie-chic (Act Two).

CONNIE OLSEN – Twenty-three, blonde, blue-eyed all-American of Scandinavian descent. Married for two years. Nine months pregnant and about to "burst," in more ways than one. Her husband, Skip, is an award-winning shoe salesman at JCPenney. Skip is never home, so Connie dreams. Hairdo: short bob. Fashion sense: maternity... sailor's outfits with matching hats and uncomfortable patent-leather heels (Act One), traditional West Indian garb (Act Two).

AGNES CROOKSHANK – Twenty-three and single. Olive-skinned and sexy/sultry. She wants to "be somebody" and fancies herself "too big for the small-town mentality." She loves to sing, act, and dance. Hairdo: glamorous. Fashion sense: Brigitte Bardot (Act One), Sophia Loren (Act Two).

DOTTIE O'FARRELL – Twenty-five, Catholic, and married to her high school sweetheart in a shotgun wedding at seventeen. She already has four children. Two more in Act Two. Her husband, Jim, is a repairman for Bell Telephone. She's forever on the latest fad diet. Hairdo: teased to the max. Fashion sense: none (Act One), still none (Act Two).

SETTING

Act One
Joan's home, 1957
A kitchen/den.

Act Two
Joan's home, 1967

The same kitchen/den transformed to reflect style changes ten years later.

AUTHOR'S NOTE

The four-piece band is made up of four women: bass, guitar, piano, and drums. The band is onstage but hidden behind the scrim. They are revealed in the second half of the show.

SONG LIST

Cookin'
Dear Abby
Didja Hear?
New Trier Fight Song
Just in Case
I'm Outta Here
Happy Hour
Somethin's Burnin'
In Limbo
Ya Dig?
Ten Years
Just a Mom
The Whomp
Blessing in Disguise
Food
In Time
Bows / The Whomp – Reprise

ACT ONE

(Joan Smith's house; Winnetka, Illinois; 1957.)

[MUSIC NO. 01 "PRE-COOKIN'"]

(The house lights fade. The curtain rises on a mid-century-style kitchen. Black and white tile floor with splashes of vibrant color and all the latest trendy gadgets.)

(During the music we reveal a poised, quintessential 1950s housewife. It is **JOAN SMITH** *in her home, wearing yellow dishwashing gloves and writing in her journal. In preparation for the day she darts to the sink, where she fills up a vase with water. As she waits for the vase to fill, she takes a sip of coffee, turns the water off, and puts the flowers into the vase. She smells the flowers, then picks up the* Betty Crocker Cookbook *on the final chord of the music.)*

JOAN. I'm Joan Smith and this *(Referring to the cookbook.)* is Betty Crocker.

> *(Music starts up again.)*

Her illustrated cookbook. In book sales, second only to the Bible! But to every woman I knew, it *WAS* the Bible. The gals in my cooking club lived by it.

> *(Beat.)*

1957. Winnetka, Illinois. 209 Cooper Lane. My home. My husband: Bob Smith. Traveling salesman. Vacation packages.

The story begins right here with our Wednesday Winnetka Women's Cooking Club. Just like clockwork. Every Wednesday. One p.m. sharp.

(The doorbell rings. **JOAN** *quickly stashes her private notebook away. She opens the front door. A very pregnant woman,* **CONNIE OLSEN***, dressed in a navy blue sailor-themed maternity ensemble, enters. She has an overflowing shopping bag full of cooking ingredients. She is walking and wobbling as a pregnant woman in high heels would.)*

JOAN. Connie!

CONNIE. Joan!

JOAN. Kick off those heels!

CONNIE. They help me keep my balance.

(Freeze. Lights on **JOAN** *as she takes* **CONNIE***'s grocery bag away from her and reveals her very pregnant belly.)*

JOAN. *(To audience.)* Connie Olsen. Due in three days. Husband: Skip. Head of women's shoes at JCPenney. Both all-American blondes. Perfect noses. She's my best friend. Don't tell the others.

(Lights up. Unfreeze.)

(Doorbell rings. **AGNES CROOKSHANK** *enters, blowing on her just-polished red nails, dressed in a push-up bra and tight orange sweater, her hair in curlers and a silk scarf around her neck. She has a small bag of ingredients.)*

*(***JOAN** *goes to hug her.)*

AGNES. Careful! My nails are wet.

JOAN & CONNIE. Agnes!

JOAN. What's with the curlers?

AGNES. I have a date tonight.

JOAN. *(Suspiciously.)* Really?

AGNES. No. But I wanted everyone in the A&P to think I did.

(Freeze. Lights on **JOAN***.)*

JOAN. *(To audience.)* Agnes Crookshank. Single. Terrible cook. But I don't care. She's great material. She's my best friend. Don't tell the others.

> *(Lights up. Unfreeze.)*

> *(Doorbell rings.* **DOTTIE O'FARRELL** *bolts through the door. She is wearing a polka-dot dress and carrying a grocery bag of cooking ingredients and a candy-striped hula hoop. She throws down all her stuff.)*

CONNIE, JOAN & AGNES. Dottie!

DOTTIE. You wouldn't believe my morning. Ronnie fell out of a tree, Johnny was eating Play-Doh, Harriet had a bead stuck up her nose and Davey put the cat in the freezer.

> (**CONNIE***'s baby kicks.*)

CONNIE. *(Grabbing belly.)* Can't wait.

DOTTIE. Your first baby. Your whole life is about to change.

> *(Freeze. Lights on* **JOAN**.*)*

JOAN. *(To audience.)* Dottie O'Farrell. Baby machine. Husband: Jim. Telephone repairman. She lives two streets over. She's my best friend. Don't tell the others.

> *(Lights up. Unfreeze.)*

Let's get cookin'!

[MUSIC NO. 02 "COOKIN'"]

JOAN.

WE MAY NOT ALL BE FIVE-STAR CHEFS

CONNIE.

BUT WE DO OUR BEST

DOTTIE.

ON THIS MIDWEST CUL-DE-SAC

AGNES.

ON THIS DEAD-END STREET

DOTTIE.

SO SWEET!

ALL.

> BUT HEY YOU NEVER KNOW WHAT YOU GET WHEN YOU
>   TURN UP THE HEAT!
>
> WHOA! WHOA!
> WE'RE COOKIN' YOU KNOW WE'RE COOKIN' SOMETHIN' UP
> WE'RE REALLY COOKIN'
> YOU KNOW WE REALLY GOT THE STUFF
> TO BE COOKIN'
> AND EACH WEEK SOMETHING NEW
> AH OOH!
> BUT BEFORE WE START COOKIN' TELL ME
> WHAT'S COOKIN' WITH YOU?

AGNES.

> LOOK!

CONNIE, JOAN & DOTTIE.

> LOOK!

AGNES.

> WHAT I GOT!

CONNIE, JOAN & DOTTIE.

> WHATCHA GOT?

AGNES.

> IT'S SO CHEAP!

CONNIE, JOAN & DOTTIE.

> IT'S SO CHEAP!

AGNES.

> IT'S A STEAL!

CONNIE, JOAN & DOTTIE.

> IT'S A STEAL!

AGNES.

> IT'S A MEAL!

CONNIE, JOAN & DOTTIE.

> IT'S A MEAL!

AGNES.

> FROM A BOX!

CONNIE, JOAN & DOTTIE.

> FROM A BOX!

AGNES.

AND IT'S GOOD!

CONNIE, JOAN & DOTTIE.

AND IT'S GOOD!

AGNES.

SO GREAT!

CONNIE, JOAN & DOTTIE.

SO GREAT!

AGNES.

JUST OPEN IT UP

CONNIE, JOAN & DOTTIE.

WOOHOO!!

AGNES.

AND THROW IT ON A PLATE!

CONNIE, JOAN & DOTTIE.

WHOA!

ALL.

COOKIN'

JOAN.

YOU KNOW WE'RE COOKIN' SOMETHIN' UP WE'RE REALLY

ALL.

COOKIN'

JOAN.

YOU KNOW WE REALLY GOT THE STUFF TO BE

ALL.

COOKIN'

JOAN.

AND EACH WEEK SOMETHIN' NEW

DOTTIE, CONNIE & AGNES.

COOKIN'

ALL.

AH OOH!

JOAN.	**CONNIE, AGNES & DOTTIE.**
BUT BEFORE WE START	COOKIN'
COOKIN'	

JOAN.	CONNIE, AGNES & DOTTIE.
TELL ME WHAT'S COOKIN'	COOKIN'
WITH YOU?	COOKIN'

CONNIE & DOTTIE.
SIFTER, LADLE
ROLLING PIN

AGNES & JOAN.
THIS TIME WE ARE
GONNA WIN

ALL.
THIS WEEK WE WILL START FROM SCRATCH
BETTY CROCKER, MEET YOUR MATCH!

JOAN. *(Reading from* Life *magazine.)* Okay, everybody, listen up! Fresh off the newsstand!

DOTTIE. What's the contest?

CONNIE. What are the prizes?

JOAN. Betty Crocker cooking contest number seventeen – "The International Flair."
(She reads.) "First prize: fifty thousand dollars in cash."

ALL.
COOKIN'!

DOTTIE. Divided by four! I could build my dream bomb shelter!

AGNES. I could buy a Corvette and drive to New York City!

CONNIE. I could book a first-class ticket. Pan Am to Trinidad!

(The others look at her.)

JOAN, DOTTIE & AGNES. TRINIDAD?!

DOTTIE. Connie! Stop dreaming, you're having a baby. You're not going anywhere, for a very, very, very long time.

CONNIE. *(Reading over* JOAN*'s shoulder.)* "Second prize, a trip to Miami."

ALL.
COOKIN'!

CONNIE. "Three nights and four days at the brand-new Fontainebleau Hotel."

ALL. Ooh.

CONNIE. "Third prize, a twelve-inch television set. Color!"

ALL.

COOKIN'!

DOTTIE. Jack Paar in color. All twelve inches.

JOAN. *(Reading on.)* "Betty Crocker International Flair Cooking Contest. Menu must include four courses – All entries must be postmarked by five p.m., June nineteenth." *[Each performance insert actual show date.]*

CONNIE, DOTTIE & AGNES. That's today!

JOAN.

FLOUR, SALT, BAKING POWDER, EGGS

CONNIE.

CHEEZ WHIZ!

JOAN.

OIL, BUTTER, SUGAR, MILK, CREAM

DOTTIE.

NECCO WAFERS!

JOAN.

POTATOES, MACARONI, BREAD CRUMBS

AGNES.

VODKA!

ALL.

CANNED CORN, CANNED BEANS, CANNED HAM CHECK!

DOTTIE.	AGNES.	CONNIE.	JOAN.
WEDNESDAY! WEDNESDAY	LOOK WHAT I GOT!	SIFTER	WE MAY NOT ALL BE
IS BEST FRIENDS	IT'S SO CHEAP!	LADLE	FIVE-STAR CHEFS, BUT WE
DAY!	IT'S A STEAL!	ROLLING	DO OUR BEST ON THIS
LOOKIN' AT OUR COOKIN'	IT'S A MEAL!	PIN	MIDWEST CUL-DE-SAC

DOTTIE.	AGNES.	CONNIE.	JOAN.
LOOKIN' GOOD!	FROM A BOX!	THIS TIME	
	AND IT'S GOOD!	WE ARE	ON THIS DEAD-END STREET
EACH WEEK	SO GREAT!	GONNA	SO SWEET
SOMETHIN' NEW! BUT	JUST	WIN. COME	BUT
BEFORE WE START COOKIN' TELL ME	OPEN IT UP	ON LET'S GET ON	HEY YOU NEVER KNOW WHAT YOU'LL GET
WHAT'S COOKIN' WITH YOU?	AND THROW IT ON A	WITH THE SHOW, BETTY	WHEN YOU TURN UP THE HEAT!
	PLATE!	CROCKER HERE WE GO!	

ALL.

COOKIN' YOU KNOW WE'RE COOKIN' SOMETHIN' UP
WE'RE REALLY COOKIN'
YOU KNOW WE'VE REALLY GOT THE STUFF
TO BE COOKIN' AND EACH WEEK SOMETHING NEW
AH OOH!
BUT BEFORE WE START COOKIN' TELL ME WHAT'S
COOKIN' WITH YOU?

DOTTIE. C'mon girls! Let's win this thing!

Four courses! That's a lot! Plus tasting. We have to taste the dishes too!

(**JOAN** *opens her notebook and scribbles in it.*)

JOAN. Okay, ideas for canapés?

CONNIE. *(Rummaging through her purse.)* A Ritz cracker with a squirt of Cheez Whiz with a sardine and a gherkin on top.

DOTTIE. Yep, girls. She's pregnant.

AGNES. How about something with a toothpick? Like little cocktail weenies?

CONNIE. Swedish meatballs? Skip's favorite. The sauce is easy. A jar of grape jelly and a bottle of ketchup.

JOAN. Anybody else? Swedish meatballs, going once, going twice...

DOTTIE. A pu-pu platter! It's Polynesian.

ALL. Oooh!

DOTTIE. When Jim came home from Korea, all he could talk about was pu-pu platters. Spare ribs, wontons, egg rolls...little bites of everything. I learned how to make crab rangoon! Do we have fresh crab?

JOAN. It's in the cabinet.

DOTTIE. Great! I can make plum sauce to go with it! It's just sugar, apple sauce, and red and blue food coloring.

JOAN. Pu-pu platter it is!

CONNIE. What about the entrée?

AGNES. How 'bout something French sounding? Shrimp dijon?

CONNIE, DOTTIE & JOAN. Ooooh!

CONNIE. Are you actually going to be cooking today, Agnes?

AGNES. I'm an idea person.

(**JOAN** *jots something down.*)

JOAN. I like it. Shrimp dijon. That's our entrée. Palate cleanser?

DOTTIE. Pretzel Jell-O mold.

CONNIE. That's not international.

DOTTIE. We'll use the Bavarian pretzels. I saw them right on the Lazy Susan, behind the Crisco.

JOAN. Okay, idea lady. Dessert?

AGNES. That cake. With the fruit on it. You know. You flip it over.

DOTTIE & CONNIE. Pineapple upside-down cake!

JOAN. Pineapples are international. They're from the island of Hawaii.

Hawaii. I haven't been there since my honeymoon with Bob.

(Gasps.)

Bob! I have to get my rump roast in the oven for Bob! He likes it on the table when he walks in the door.

CONNIE. Skip hates my rump roast. I've tried over and over again.

DOTTIE. You have to pound it so the meat becomes tender. Jim loves that.

JOAN. (Reading on.) Okay last but not least. It says we need a "colorful cocktail with an international theme."

AGNES. Cocktails are my department.

JOAN. (Reading on.) Let's think. Hmmm. "International."

(**AGNES** holds up a bottle.)

AGNES. Well, how 'bout Seagram's Vodka? It says it's from Canada!

(**JOAN** takes the bottle from **AGNES**.)

JOAN. You know what, Agnes? Let's decide on the cocktail later. Girls I feel good about this contest, don't you?

DOTTIE. Yes. We weren't on our game for the other sixteen. But they say seventeen's the charm!

AGNES. And this is our last contest for awhile.

DOTTIE. Because someone's got a little bun in the oven!

CONNIE. My due date is this Saturday!

JOAN. (Reading from her notes.) Agnes – help Dottie with the pu-pus.

DOTTIE. I don't need help with my pu-pus.

AGNES. I'll boil the water for the Jell-O.

DOTTIE. You'll probably ruin that.

AGNES. Fine, Dottie. I'll just be the pretty one.

DOTTIE. Yes. Pretty and single.

AGNES. Sounds good to me.

CONNIE. Tone it down girls. You're upsetting the baby.

JOAN. Team effort. Hands in.

ALL. Wednesday Winnetka Women.

(Hands in for a "team break.")

WOO –

(Ding! They freeze, hands in the air.)

[MUSIC NO. 02A "WEDNESDAY WINNETKA WOMEN (WOO!)"]

(Lights on JOAN.)

JOAN. *(To audience.)* Dottie, Connie, Agnes, my best friends. We could say anything to each other. The kitchen was a sacred place. It all happened right here. We cooked and in between cooking, we bickered, laughed, cried and tried to figure out life. We were being fed a lot of notions about our place in the world. We were told one thing but we felt another. And there were very few places we could go for advice.

(Lights up. They unfreeze and "team break.")

ALL. – HOO!!

AGNES. *(Reading paper.)* "Dear Abby – My husband comes home late every night and tells me he's been working overtime at the office. I know he loves me, but yesterday I had to bleach a lipstick stain off the collar of his shirt...again. We have three kids and I can't bear to lose him. What to do? Signed, Clorox in Cleveland."

JOAN. Shocking.

CONNIE. Is it?

JOAN. Poor thing.

AGNES. She should just talk to her husband.

JOAN. She should talk to a psychiatrist.

CONNIE. But then everyone would think she was crazy.

DOTTIE. I would never tell my secrets to a stranger.

(They ad-lib. Bell tone. Spotlight.)

[MUSIC NO. 03 "DEAR ABBY"]

DEAR ABBY

JOAN.

ABBY

AGNES.

ABBY

CONNIE.

ABBY

DOTTIE.   **JOAN, AGNES & CONNIE.**

TELL ME, HAVE YOU GOT   AAH
ANY TRICKS

JOAN.

ABBY

AGNES.

ABBY

CONNIE.

ABBY

DOTTIE.   **JOAN, AGNES & CONNIE.**

GIVE ME A QUICK AND   AAH
EASY FIX

JOAN, AGNES & CONNIE.

QUICK AND EASY FIX

DOTTIE.

SO WEDNESDAY I'LL WAKE UP AND BE SIZE SIX

(They unfold a newspaper with a picture of a woman in a bikini.)

JOAN, AGNES & CONNIE.

GIVE HER SOME TRICKS TO BE SIZE SIX

*(**AGNES** in spotlight.)*

AGNES.

OH, DEAR ABBY

JOAN.

ABBY

DOTTIE.

ABBY

CONNIE.

ABBY

AGNES.

I'M SO UNHAPPY I COULD
    CRY

JOAN, CONNIE & DOTTIE.

AAH

JOAN.

ABBY

DOTTIE.

ABBY

CONNIE.

ABBY

AGNES.

I HAVE MUCH BIGGER
    FISH TO FRY

JOAN, CONNIE & DOTTIE.

AAH

JOAN, CONNIE & DOTTIE.

BIGGER FISH TO FRY

AGNES.

IF ANN-MARGRET MADE IT, TELL ME WHY CAN'T I?

JOAN, CONNIE & DOTTIE.

NOT WITH A NAME LIKE AGNES

DOTTIE.

THEY SAY TRUE BEAUTY'S
    ON THE INSIDE
AND THAT'S WHAT REALLY
    COUNTS

JOAN & CONNIE.

OOO, SHOOP DOO-WAH

SHOOP DOO-WAH

AGNES.

BUT I WANT MORE

DOTTIE.

BUT I WANT MORE

JOAN & CONNIE.

SHOOP DO-WAH
SHOOP DO-WAH
SHOOP DO-WAH

AGNES.

THAN WATCHING TIME
    FLY BY
BAKING YET ANOTHER PIE

JOAN & CONNIE.

SHOOP DOO-WAH

DOTTIE.

OR HIDING HERSHEY'S IN
    THE BOTTOM DRAWER

JOAN & CONNIE.

SHOOP DOO-WAH

JOAN.

OOO

AGNES.

OOO

DOTTIE.

OOO

CONNIE.

OOO

ALL.

ABBY I NEED YOU, SHOOP SHOOP DOO-WAH
ABBY I NEED YOU, SHOOP SHOOP DOO-WAH
ABBY I NEED YOU, SHOOP SHOOP DOO-WAH
DEAR ABBY

JOAN. Ya know, Abby isn't her real name.

DEAR PAULINE ESTHER FRIEDMAN

AGNES.

PAULINE

DOTTIE.

ESTHER

CONNIE.

FRIEDMAN

JOAN.	**AGNES, CONNIE & DOTTIE.**
I WANT A COLUMN JUST LIKE YOU	AAH

AGNES.

PAULINE

DOTTIE.

ESTHER

CONNIE.

FRIEDMAN

JOAN.	**AGNES, CONNIE & DOTTIE.**
EVERY DAY HELPING US GET THROUGH	AAH

AGNES.

PAULINE

DOTTIE.

ESTHER

CONNIE.

    FRIEDMAN

JOAN.	**AGNES, CONNIE & DOTTIE.**
BY TELLING US EXACTLY	AAH
WHAT TO DO	

JOAN, AGNES & DOTTIE.

    ABBY I NEED YOU, ABBY I NEED YOU, ABBY I NEED YOU

CONNIE.	**AGNES & DOTTIE.**
I REALLY WANT THIS BABY	OOP SHOO WAH
CAN I TRUST MYSELF	OOP SHOO WAH

CONNIE & JOAN.

    TO FOLLOW MY HEART?
    OOP OOP SHOO WAH
    OOP SHOO WAH

AGNES.

    I WANNA BE SOMEBODY

CONNIE & JOAN.

    OOP OOP SHOO WAH

DOTTIE.

    IN A POLKA-DOT BIKINI

ALL.

    GEE, ABBY YOU'RE SO SMART
    OH, DEAR ABBY
    MAYBE I'LL NEVER SEND A LETTER
    BUT SAYING IT OUT LOUD MADE ME FEEL BETTER
    ABIGAIL VAN BUREN, YOU'RE THE BEST
    SIGNED,

DOTTIE.

    FAT

AGNES.

    TRAPPED

JOAN.

    OY

CONNIE.

    (BURP)

ALL.

    IN ILLINOIS

JOAN. Okay everybody, to your stations! Agnes and I will work on the shrimp dijon. Dottie, you've got pu-pus over there, and Connie, in the middle.

(*They start preparing.*)

DOTTIE. Connie, have you put the finishing touches on the nursery yet?

CONNIE. Yes we just got done painting little ducks on the walls. And since we don't know what it's going be, Skip and I both knitted pink and blue blankets.

DOTTIE. Skip?

CONNIE. Yes. He's loved knitting ever since he was a little boy.

DOTTIE. You're so lucky. I can't get Jim to change a diaper. Does he iron?

JOAN. Are you going to breastfeed?

CONNIE. Aah! Joan, shhhh.

JOAN. It's my house, Connie. No one's home. I can say breast.

CONNIE & DOTTIE. Aah!

AGNES. Breast. Breast. Breast. Breast. Breast. Boobies!

CONNIE & DOTTIE. Aah!

DOTTIE. Stop saying that. It's not ladylike.

JOAN. What's more ladylike than a breast?

DOTTIE. Besides, it's better to bottle-feed anyhow. That's what they say now. I wish I'd known.

AGNES. Who's "they"?

DOTTIE. You know, "them."

CONNIE. I want my figure back. I haven't seen my toes in three months.

AGNES. Well, "they" also say that breastfeeding can ruin your figure forever.

(*Looking at* **DOTTIE**.) Just because you have a baby you shouldn't let yourself go.

DOTTIE. We all weren't meant to be prom queens like Connie.

JOAN. Remember your gorgeous gown, Connie? Hot pink.

AGNES. I had my gown already picked out. But I guess blondes are more popular.

CONNIE. Okay, if you're going to bring that up again, Agnes, let's talk about what happened with my prom king.

JOAN. Here we go.

> (*Lights on* **JOAN**. *Ding! The others freeze.*)

[MUSIC NO. 03A "PROM KING"]

(*To audience.*) Senior year. Biff Qually. Quarterback.

> (*Lights up. Unfreeze.*)

CONNIE. (*Looking at* **AGNES**.) When it came time for the king and queen's dance, who was left standing alone when the band started to play "Mona Lisa"? Me. Why?

DOTTIE. Because the prom king was necking under the bleachers with you know who.

AGNES. He started it.

JOAN. (*Amusedly.*) Agnes, did you boff Biff?

AGNES. I plead the fifth.

AGNES & JOAN. Hey, that rhymes!

Jinx! You owe me a Coke!

CONNIE. (*To* **AGNES**.) And you owe me a prom king.

AGNES. Move on. You're about to have Skip's baby.

> (**CONNIE** *bursts into tears.*)

DOTTIE. This is why we lose every contest. We bicker instead of cook.

> (**DOTTIE** *hands* **CONNIE** *a pretzel.*)

Here.

CONNIE. I'll be fine.

JOAN. This week, maybe we should try to cook without talking.

> (*They try for a minute.*)

[MUSIC NO. 04 "DIDJA HEAR?"]

DOTTIE. Didja hear –

JOAN. *(Cutting her off.)* And without gossiping.

DOTTIE. It's not gossip. It's news.

AGNES. If we don't gossip, what are we gonna do?

DOTTIE. It is our civic duty to know what's happening with
our neighbors. I'm just doing my part.

JOAN. Okay, whadja hear?

DOTTIE.

> I WAS ROLLIN' AROUND
> THE GROCERY STORE
> THREE AISLES FROM THE SOUP

CONNIE, AGNES & JOAN.

> THE SOUP

DOTTIE.

> NOW YOU KNOW ME, I KEEP TO MYSELF
> I'VE NEVER BEEN ONE TO SNOOP

CONNIE, AGNES & JOAN.

> TO SNOOP

DOTTIE.

> I WAS MINDING MY OWN BUSINESS

CONNIE, AGNES & JOAN.

> UH-HUH...

DOTTIE.

> IT'S NOT LIKE I REALLY CARE

CONNIE, AGNES & JOAN.

> RIGHT

DOTTIE.

> BUT DID YOU KNOW THAT TOM AND JANE AND DICK
> ARE HAVING AN AFFAIR?

CONNIE, AGNES & JOAN.

> NO!

DOTTIE.

> DIDJA HEAR?
> DIDJA HEAR?

JOAN.

> WHO?

CONNIE.

> WHA'DIDJA HEAR?

CONNIE, AGNES & JOAN.

COME ON TELL US WHA'DIDJA SEE?

DOTTIE.

IF THEY ASK WHERE'DJA HEAR?

AND YOU DID

YA GOTTA SWEAR

YA DIDN'T HEAR IT FROM ME

CONNIE.

I WAS SITTIN' ON A STOOL AT THE REXALL COUNTER

HAVIN' A ROOT BEER FLOAT

AGNES, DOTTIE & JOAN.

ROOT BEER FLOAT

CONNIE.

BEHIND THE MAYBELLINE AND THE AQUA NET

I SAW EDDIE G SLIP JOHNNY P A NOTE

INTO HIS COAT

AGNES, DOTTIE & JOAN.

SO?

CONNIE.

JUST A RUMOR...I SHOULDN'T MENTION IT

AGNES, DOTTIE & JOAN.

COME ON!

CONNIE.

BUT OKAY, IF YOU INSIST

AGNES, DOTTIE & JOAN.

WE INSIST!

CONNIE.

I'M NOT SAYING THAT IT'S TRUE

BUT YOU KNOW WHO IS A COMMUNIST!

AGNES, DOTTIE & JOAN.

A RED?

ALL.

DIDJA HEAR?

DIDJA HEAR?

WHA'DIDJA HEAR?

COME ON TELL US WHA'DIDJA SEE?

IF THEY ASK WHERE'DJA HEAR?

AND YA DID

YA GOTTA SWEAR
YA DIDN'T HEAR IT FROM ME

DOTTIE.

GLORIA TOLD SHIRLEY
WHO TOLD ETHEL
WHO TOLD BABS

CONNIE.

WHO TOLD GLADYS
WHO TOLD PEGGY

AGNES.

WHO YOU KNOW ALWAYS BLABS

JOAN.

AND NOW I'M TELLING YOU
SO THAT'S A CLUE

ALL.

IT'S GOTTA BE TRUE

AGNES.

GET THIS GIRLS!
I WAS PULLIN' INTO THE ESSO ON MAIN
PICKIN' UP A PACK OF LUCKY STRIKES

(Pulls the pack out of her bra.)

DOTTIE, CONNIE & JOAN.

FILTERLESS!
OUT OF THE CORNER OF HER EYE
SHE SAW FATHER O'NEILL

AGNES.

STUMBLIN' OUT OF DIRTY MIKE'S

ALL. (**DOTTIE** *crosses herself.*)

OH GOD!

JOAN.

GIRLS, WE'VE WASTED FIFTEEN MINUTES

CONNIE, DOTTIE & AGNES.

WHOOPS!

JOAN.

WITH ALL THIS DRIVEL AND CRAP

CONNIE, DOTTIE & AGNES.

IT'S NOT CRAP!

JOAN.

BUT I WAS UNDER THE DRYER AT JACQUES DU PARIS
WHEN I READ CLARK KENT'S GOT THE CLAP

DOTTIE.

TELL LOIS!

ALL.

DIDJA HEAR?
DIDJA HEAR?
WHA'DIDJA HEAR?
COME ON TELL US WHA'DIDJA SEE?
IF THEY ASK WHERE'DJA HEAR?
AND YOU DID
YA GOTTA SWEAR
YA DIDN'T HEAR IT FROM
YA DIDN'T HEAR IT FROM

DOTTIE.

GLORIA, SHIRLEY, ETHEL, BABS
GLADYS AND PEGGY WHO ALWAYS BLABS

ALL.

YA DIDN'T HEAR IT FROM ME!

*(Not interested in cooking, **AGNES** leaves her station and picks up the* Life *magazine.)*

AGNES. I love Wednesdays. It's when I catch up on all my Hollywood stars. And my horoscope!
Joan is this a new table? So shiny! I can see myself in it!

*(**AGNES** re-applies her lipstick while looking down at her reflection in the tabletop.)*

JOAN. No, same old table. Bob was at Ace Hardware buying car wax and found a Turtle Wax product to use on furniture. Looks good right? He uses Turtle Wax on the Crestline and I use it on the Formica!

*(**AGNES** finishes with the lipstick and starts reading her magazine.)*

AGNES. That's impressive. Well, let me know if you need anything.

DOTTIE. Agnes, Joe Bonomo says if you don't know how to cook, you can't win a man.

(*Ding! They freeze.*)

[MUSIC NO. 04A "YOU CAN'T WIN A MAN"]

(**JOAN** *takes a little book out of Dottie's purse and turns to the audience.*)

(*She starts out writing and gets up to finish with a direct address to the audience:*)

JOAN. (*Reads to audience.*) "Pull up a chair, Ladies." That's how he starts every book. *Essential Tips For Every Woman* by Joe Bonomo. Crazy, but these were real. Right next to the gum and mints at the checkout counter. Some of us listened. Some of us laughed. But I guarantee you, in every purse in Winnetka was at least one of these handy pocket manuals. Every purse except Agnes'.

(**JOAN** *puts the book back in Dottie's purse. The others unfreeze.*)

AGNES. Okay, Joe Bonomo, what does a man have to do to win a woman?

DOTTIE. With those kinds of questions, Agnes, you'll never win one.

(**CONNIE** *grabs the pocket manual.*)

CONNIE. Listen up, Agnes. *How to Find Your Man and Hold Him – Ten Easy Steps to the Altar.* Number one: Prepare mentally.

DOTTIE. Exactly. Number two: Sometimes you must put on an act.

CONNIE. If you need to.

DOTTIE. Number three: Is your outfit a complement to his?

JOAN. It was, when we were skinny-dipping in Waikiki.

(*Reactions from the others.*)

DOTTIE. Fresh!

AGNES. Tell me, why can't a woman become somebody without a man?

DOTTIE. Who would want to?

CONNIE. That would be a heck of a lot of work.

DOTTIE. *(Pulling a manual out of her bra.)* Well I live by the *Bonomo Housekeeping Manual.*

CONNIE. *(Pulls one out of her bra.)* I've got that one too!

CONNIE & DOTTIE. "Simplify Your Housekeeping."

DOTTIE. "Techniques for Making Housekeeping an Art."

AGNES. Hire a maid.

CONNIE. "How to Win Compliments on Your Housekeeping."

AGNES. Hire a French maid.

DOTTIE. "Are You Equipped to Keep Home?"

AGNES. Depends on the maid.

DOTTIE. You shouldn't be joking about this, Agnes! You're twenty-three! Practically a spinster.

AGNES. Maybe I want to be single. Maybe I don't want four screaming little brats running around.

DOTTIE. Hey you can't call my kids brats! Only I can. That's the joy of motherhood.

JOAN. *(Warding off a fight.)* You know Agnes, Bob has a friend he works with that would be perfect for you.

> *(**AGNES** sees* Life *magazine with Rock Hudson on the cover and picks it up.)*

AGNES. No offense, but I've met Bob's friends.

> *(She snores.)*

I want Rock Hudson.

DOTTIE. You had your chance, Agnes, but now he's a big movie star.

CONNIE. Do you believe a boy from our high school is now "the most eligible bachelor in the world"?

DOTTIE. *(Looking at the picture.)* That bandana is so neat! He and my older brother Buck were like this.

> (*Crosses her fingers to show everyone how "tight" they were.*)

DOTTIE. How did they come up with the name "ROCK HUDSON" from Roy Scherer from New Trier?

CONNIE. Ready? Okay!

CONNIE & DOTTIE. New Trier High School!

[MUSIC NO. 04B "NEW TRIER FIGHT SONG"]

DOTTIE.
> HERE'S TO OUR TEAM, WE'RE THE GREEN AND THE GREY!
> MAY WE ALWAYS HAIL!

CONNIE & DOTTIE.
> FIGHTING TO WIN, WE ARE FAITHFUL AND BRAVE
> AND MAY WE NEVER FAIL!
> JOIN IN CHEERS FOR OUR TEAM
> MAKING HISTORY
> LOYAL FANS OF NEW TRIER WE WILL ALWAYS BE!

ALL.
> IN ALL THAT WE DO
> WE ARE FAITHFUL AND TRUE
> SINGING RAH RAH! FOR OLD NEW TRIER!

DOTTIE. (*Referring to herself.*) Yup! Still got it.

CONNIE. Oh, it's been years since we've cheered together!

JOAN. Are we cheering or chopping?

DOTTIE. We're chopping, we're chopping.

> (**DOTTIE** *goes to her purse and takes out a box of Good & Plenty candy.*)

JOAN. Dottie, your diet. You asked me to keep you accountable.

DOTTIE. I'm on the "Eat All You Want and Lose Weight" diet. You take these pills before you eat all you want and one after you eat all you want.

CONNIE. I don't think it works with Good & Plenty.

DOTTIE. (*With a mouthful.*) It's a special occasion.

JOAN. What occasion?

DOTTIE. Wednesday. Joan, do you have any Coca-Cola? I need to wash down my pill.

> (**JOAN** *gets a Coke from the fridge.*)
>
> (*Suddenly, what sounds like an air raid siren goes off.*)

Duck and cover!!

> (*The women hold on to each other for dear life and "duck and cover" under the table. In the commotion,* **DOTTIE** *grabs her purse upside down and its contents explode all over the floor. Pill bottles are rolling everywhere.*)

CONNIE. Dottie, I think that's an ambulance, not an air raid siren!

JOAN. (*Reading labels.*) Dexedrine, Compazine, Imipramine –

DOTTIE. My S&H Green Stamp book!

AGNES. Elavil, Tuinal, Seconal –

DOTTIE. Only two hundred fifty-three more licks to get to the Ozarks!

CONNIE. (*Continuing.*) Miltown, Darvon –

DOTTIE. (*Discovering.*) There's my Dippity-Do.

JOAN. Dottie?! You're hopped up on drugs!

DOTTIE. What? My doctors prescribed each and every one of them. It's medicine! For all of my...conditions.

JOAN. What conditions?

CONNIE. You're a healthy twenty-five-year-old woman.

DOTTIE. Well, you know. Just in case.

[MUSIC NO. 05 "JUST IN CASE"]

THERE'S A PILL FOR EV'RY BUMP AND BRUISE
OR WHEN YOU NEED A SNOOZE
JUST IN CASE

THERE'S ONE TO LIFT YOU UP OR DROP YOU DOWN
OR IF YOUR MOTHER-IN-LAW'S IN TOWN
IN CASE

IF THERE IS A PIMPLE ON YOUR FACE

OR MAYBE YOU JUST WANNA WIN A RACE

YOU NEVER KNOW WHEN YOU WILL NEED 'EM
KEEP 'EM IN SAFE PLACE
JUST IN CASE

AGNES, JOAN & CONNIE.

IN CASE?

DOTTIE.

IF YOU WANNA LOSE A LITTLE WEIGHT
I HAVE THESE BLUE ONES HANDY
JUST

> (**AGNES, JOAN,** *and* **CONNIE** *are asking,* **DOTTIE**
> *is telling:*)

AGNES, JOAN, CONNIE & DOTTIE.

IN CASE?

DOTTIE.

THEY'RE WONDERFUL, I'M FEELING SO ALIVE
I TOOK FIVE! THEY'RE LIKE CANDY!
CHARLIE SAYS I LOVE MY GOOD 'N PLENTY
CHARLIE SAYS IT REALLY RINGS THE BELL

DING!

CHARLIE SAYS I LOVE MY GOOD 'N PLENTY
DON'T KNOW ANY OTHER CANDY THAT I LOVE SO WELL!

AGNES, JOAN & CONNIE.

WHAT'CHA DOIN'? WHAT'CHA DOIN'?
YOU'RE INSANE!

DOTTIE.

BUT WHAT IF YOU FALL DOWN AND BREAK A HEEL?

AGNES, JOAN & CONNIE. *(They agree with her.)*

SO?

DOTTIE.

OR THERE'S A FEELING YOU DON'T WANNA FEEL

AGNES, JOAN & CONNIE. *(They agree with her.)*

OH.

DOTTIE.

IF YOU'VE LOST YOUR MIND, YOUR KEYS, YOUR PARKING
SPACE

POP ONE!

JUST IN CASE

AGNES, JOAN & CONNIE.

IN CASE!

DOTTIE. The doctor put me on these miracle diet pills! And all of a sudden I'm so peppy! And I don't mind doing the housework.

IF YOU WANNA CLEAN AND CLEAN AND CLEAN

AND CLEAN AND CLEAN BECAUSE YOU

BROKE

AGNES, JOAN & CONNIE.

THE VASE!

DOTTIE. *(Sees that they understand.)*

YES!

YOU DON'T NEED A DRINK

JUST TAKE A PINK ONE

YOU WILL THINK THAT YOU ARE PRINCESS GRACE.

A PILL CAN REALLY GET YOU IN THE MOOD

AGNES, JOAN & CONNIE.

TRUE!

DOTTIE.

WHEN YOU START TO FEEL YOU'VE COME UNGLUED

AGNES, JOAN & CONNIE.

OOO!

DOTTIE.

IF THERE IS A MEMORY YOU CAN'T ERASE

POP ONE JUST IN CASE

AGNES, JOAN & CONNIE.

IN CASE!

DOTTIE & CONNIE.

POP ONE!

AGNES & JOAN.

POP ONE!

DOTTIE & CONNIE.

DROP ONE!

AGNES & JOAN.

DROP ONE!

DOTTIE & CONNIE.
> CRUSH ONE!

AGNES & JOAN.
> CRUSH ONE?

DOTTIE & CONNIE.
> PLOP ONE!

AGNES & JOAN.
> PLOP ONE?

DOTTIE.	**AGNES, JOAN & CONNIE.**
TAKE MY ADVICE	AAH
YOU BETTER HAVE ONE!	AAH, AAH, AAH
TRUST ME!	

AGNES, JOAN & CONNIE.
> OH, MUST WE?

DOTTIE.
> JUST IN CASE!

AGNES, JOAN & CONNIE.
> IN CASE!

DOTTIE.
> YUP!

Sorry girls, I just got carried away. But if you need anything for a headache or heartburn, you know where to come.

CONNIE. *(Desperately.)* I don't need a pill. I need a coconut.

JOAN. What?

DOTTIE. She's craving coconut!

JOAN. Right now?

CONNIE. Right now.

DOTTIE. Right now!

> *(They put their coats on and scramble to go out the door.)*

Wait! Where are we going to find a coconut in Winnetka? Come on back!

> *(They all come back.)*

I've got an Almond Joy in my purse!

CONNIE. I'll take it.

>*(**DOTTIE** throws her the candy bar.)*

JOAN. *(Sees the clock.)* Girls! It's three o'clock! The contest! Let's get back to cooking!

DOTTIE. My pu-pus are already in the oven so I have time to show you girls my new exercise. It's the latest craze!

>*(**DOTTIE** starts hula-hooping.)*

One calorie, two calories, three calories.

JOAN. *(Watching **DOTTIE**.)* Look at those moves. A regular Elvis Presley.

AGNES. Look! Rock is in a new movie with Sidney Poitier called *Something of Value*.

CONNIE. Sidney Poitier is so handsome.

DOTTIE. Yeah, but he's a – *(She mouths out the word "Negro.")*

CONNIE. Dottie, he's dreamy. In any color.

DOTTIE. Connie, you shouldn't even be thinking that out loud.

CONNIE. Why? It's only us. And I think he's sexy.

DOTTIE. I'm just protecting you.

JOAN. From what?

DOTTIE. Well for one thing, it's illegal in most places.

AGNES. You should be able to love whoever you want to.

>*(All freeze. **DOTTIE**'s hula hoop falls to the floor. on **JOAN** writing once again. Ding!)*

[MUSIC NO. 05A "BUBBLIN' UP IN THE KITCHEN"]

JOAN. *(To audience.)* Lots of things bubbled up in the kitchen.

Words. Opinions. New ideas. Things that were socially off-limits at cocktail parties.

Race.

Jackie Robinson broke every baseball record, but couldn't stay in the same hotel as his teammates. Even that was illegal. Sex.

You could talk about babies but not how you made 'em.

(Lights up. The others unfreeze. **CONNIE***'s baby kicks. She cries out and clutches her stomach.)*

CONNIE. Ow!

DOTTIE. *(Referring to the baby kicking.)* Already talking back!

*(****JOAN*** *tamps the pack of cigarettes on her hand, takes one out, and lights up.)*

CONNIE. Can I get a cig?

*(****JOAN*** *gives* **CONNIE** *one and then* **DOTTIE** *as well. They smoke together.)*

Thanks. Dr. Spock says smoking's good for the expectant mother 'cause it's so relaxing.

DOTTIE. *(Sincerely.)* When I was pregnant, my doctor told me to "wear a boned corset..."

CONNIE. *(Agreeing with* **DOTTIE***.)* "...To minimize your calcium intake to soften your growing baby's bones..."

CONNIE & DOTTIE. "...Making sliding out of the birth canal easier."

DOTTIE. Believe me, with twins, you want them to slide.

*(****CONNIE****'s baby kicks again.)*

CONNIE. Whoa! I guess I have to inhale more deeply.

JOAN. *(Looking at everyone's progress.)* Okay, the pu-pus and the rump roast are in the oven. The Jell-O is gelling. Girls, we have a few minutes.

DOTTIE. You know what that means!

CONNIE. Our exercises!

(With cigarettes dangling from their mouths, **CONNIE**, **DOTTIE**, *and* **JOAN** *slap the backs of their hands in rhythm under their chins to do their chin-firming exercises, followed by their "pinching their cheeks to make them rosy" exercises, followed by pressing their*

palms together for their bust exercises. **AGNES**
is still reading at the table.)

DOTTIE, CONNIE & JOAN.

(Chin-firming.) ONE AND TWO AND THREE AND
FOUR

(Cheek pinching.) ONE AND TWO AND THREE
AND FOUR

(Palms pressing together.) WE MUST, WE MUST
WE MUST INCREASE OUR BUST
THE BIGGER THE BETTER
THE TIGHTER THE SWEATER
THE BOYS DEPEND ON US

> **(AGNES** *finds a newspaper clipping in Joan's
> notebook and interrupts them.)*

AGNES. Joan! I thought you were keeping recipes in this
notebook!

CONNIE. What does it say?!

> **(DOTTIE** *grabs it from* **AGNES.***)*

DOTTIE. *(Horrified.)* I can't look at this! It's dirty!!

> **(CONNIE** *grabs it from* **DOTTIE.***)*

CONNIE. Whoa.

> **(JOAN** *grabs it back.)*

JOAN. *(To* **DOTTIE.***)* Give me that! It's research.

AGNES. *(Reads.)* "The Nifty Fifties: Today's Woman's Sex
Life..." Joan, you minx. What else are you hiding from
us?

DOTTIE. *(Covering her ears.)* I don't wanna know.

CONNIE. I do. But I understand if you want to keep it a
secret.

JOAN. It's no secret. I'm taking classes at night school. To
be a writer.

CONNIE. Of pornography?

JOAN. To be a journalist.

DOTTIE. Don't be silly. Women aren't journalists.

JOAN. I want to write important stories. Not pieces in the local paper about girdles and fishnet stockings. I'm interested in shaking things up. Talking about things people are afraid to talk about.

(**AGNES** *runs to the TV and turns it on.*)

AGNES. Good for you, Joan. At least someone has some moxie around here, besides me.

JOAN. Thank you.

AGNES. Can we move this conversation over to the TV? The *Ted Mack Amateur Hour* is on!

DOTTIE. You do this every Wednesday! We can't waste time! Fifty thousand dollars is at stake!

CONNIE. Dottie's right.

AGNES. Shh. Ann-Margret's on! It's the final round this week!

(*They look at the TV set.*)

ALL. (*In rhythm as a cheer.*) Ann-Margret Olsson from New Trier High!

AGNES. (*Shouting.*) It's between Ann and the Mexican leaf player! Somebody get me a postcard! I wanna vote for her!

DOTTIE. I do too! She was a great cheerleader!

AGNES. Yes, if Ann-Margret got out of this town, so can I! Come on, let's all vote for Ann!

(**JOAN** *hands her a postcard.*)

JOAN. I'm in.

DOTTIE. Put me down for Ann.

(**JOAN** *goes to turn the TV off.*)

CONNIE. Wait! Fill one out for me too! One vote for the Mexican leaf player.

(*The others look at her.*)

AGNES. That's not talent!

CONNIE. Remind me, what song can you play on a leaf?

DOTTIE. Do you think Betty Crocker wastes her time watching TV? No. Betty's got a business to run!

JOAN. Back to your stations.

AGNES. *(Collecting the postcards.)* Still Joan, mail the postcards with our entry.

> *(**JOAN** gathers the postcards up and continues to write.)*

> *(**AGNES** turns to the side and rips up Connie's postcard.)*

Does anybody know how I can get on that program?

JOAN. *(Fed up.)* For Pete's sake Agnes, they say it at the end of every show. You have to write to 79 Seventh Avenue, New York, New York.

DOTTIE. Why do they always say that twice?

CONNIE. You know Agnes, it wouldn't kill you to at least *try* to cook. "The way to a man's heart is through his stomach."

AGNES. I'm not interested, Connie. I have my own dreams. One day I'm gonna be a star!

DOTTIE. Oh, Agnes, don't get too big for your britches.

CONNIE. Remember when her pants split wide open at the school play when she was playing Annie Oakley?

DOTTIE. Remember? It was on the front page of the *New Trier News*!

> *(**JOAN**, **DOTTIE**, *and* **CONNIE** *laugh.*)*

[MUSIC NO. 06 "I'M OUTTA HERE"]

AGNES.
ENOUGH!
YOU KNOW ME
HAVE I EVER BEEN ABLE TO FOLLOW A RECIPE?

DOTTIE, CONNIE & JOAN. No, not really. Never. Uh-uh.

AGNES.
WHEN IT SAYS SUGAR, I ADD SPICE
WHEN IT SAYS ONCE, I SHAKE IT TWICE
WHEN YOU SAY GO WITH THE STATUS QUO

SUDDENLY IT ALL BECOMES QUITE CLEAR
I'M OUTTA HERE

DOTTIE, CONNIE & JOAN.

OOH, OOH
SHE'S OUTTA HERE

AGNES.

OOH THIS TOWN IS REALLY SQUARE
WHY CAN'T I LET DOWN MY HAIR?
GOTTA

ALL.

FEEL THE FEEL BEHIND THE WHEEL

AGNES.

AND KICK IT INTO HIGH GEAR
I'M OUTTA HERE

DOTTIE, CONNIE & JOAN.

OOH, OOH
SHE'S OUTTA HERE

AGNES.

THEY SAY A WOMAN'S ONLY DREAM SHOULD BE
HOW TO FIND THE PERFECT MAN

DOTTIE, CONNIE & JOAN.

THE PERFECT MAN

AGNES.

LOOK LIKE MARILYN,

ALL.

COOK LIKE SARA LEE

AGNES.

BUT WHAT IF A GIRL HAS ANOTHER PLAN?
I CAN SMELL

DOTTIE, CONNIE & JOAN.

SMELL

AGNES.

THAT SWEET SUCCESS

DOTTIE, CONNIE & JOAN.

THAT SWEET SUCCESS

AGNES.

I CAN TASTE

DOTTIE, CONNIE & JOAN.
TASTE

AGNES.
HOW IT'S GONNA BE

DOTTIE, CONNIE & JOAN.
HOW IT'S GONNA BE

AGNES.
I CAN SEE

DOTTIE, CONNIE & JOAN.
SEE

AGNES.
THAT SWARMING PRESS

DOTTIE, CONNIE & JOAN.
THAT SWARMING PRESS

AGNES.
I CAN TOUCH

DOTTIE, CONNIE & JOAN.
TOUCH

ALL.
THAT BIG MARQUEE

AGNES.
THAT'S ME
MARIA MAGENTA

ALL.
OVERNIGHT SENSATION!

AGNES.
I'M STEALING THE HEART

ALL.
OF THE ENTIRE NATION!

AGNES.
I CAN

ALL.
DANCE!

AGNES.
I CAN

ALL.
SING!

AGNES.

I'VE GOT

ALL.

EVERYTHING!

AGNES.	**DOTTIE, CONNIE & JOAN.**
BROADWAY'S NEWEST STAR TO APPEAR I'M OUTTA HERE!	OOO, OOO

DOTTIE, CONNIE & JOAN.

SHE'S OUTTA HERE

BYE BYE!

AGNES.

OH, I'M OUTTA HERE!

DOTTIE, CONNIE & JOAN.	**AGNES.**
SHE'S OUTTA HERE BYE BYE!	YEAH

AGNES.

OH YEAH I'M OUTTA HERE! YEAH!

DOTTIE, CONNIE & JOAN.	**AGNES.**
SHE'S OUT OF HERE BYE BYE!	OOO OOO OOO OOO OOO

AGNES.

I'M OUTTA HERE!

DOTTIE, CONNIE & JOAN.

SHE'S OUTTA HERE!

AGNES.

I'M GONE!

DOTTIE, CONNIE & JOAN.

BYE!

JOAN. So go. What's stopping you?

DOTTIE. Why would you want to leave us? All of that is a fairy tale. Don't you want something real?

AGNES. This is *your* real. I love you all, and I love our Wednesdays – but I don't belong here.

Something's missing.

JOAN. Now's the time to take a leap. You have no mortgage, no husband, and you've already saved a lot not having to pay rent at your parents' house. I say go for it!

CONNIE. Just get a credit card! You don't have to pay anything!

AGNES. I applied but was denied.

JOAN. Oh, that's right. You have to be MISSUS Agnes Crookshank to get a card. You gotta be married to go into debt.

AGNES. Now you see why we've gotta win this contest if I'm going to get to New York!

DOTTIE. And you'll need a publicity photo.

AGNES. An eight by ten glossy!

CONNIE. And I have the perfect thing for your skin!

AGNES. What's wrong with my skin?

CONNIE. Oh nothing, it's helping me fade my freckles. Joe Bonomo says freckles can cause personality problems.

(They continue prepping the shrimp dijon.)

CONNIE. How many shrimp in the shrimp dijon?

JOAN. The whole can.

CONNIE. Okay. Shrimp.

DOTTIE. Dijon.

JOAN. Mix.

AGNES. Dinner's ready!

DOTTIE. Do you think Betty Crocker tastes everything herself?

JOAN. Of course, in her test kitchen.

*(**AGNES** grabs a fork and tastes.)*

AGNES. *(Tasting the shrimp.)* Too bland. Sprinkle some Accent on it. It brings the flavor out in everything.

CONNIE. Agnes, you say that every Wednesday about every dish.

*(Takes the spice from **AGNES** and looks at it.)*

What's in this stuff anyway?

AGNE. I have no idea. It doesn't say.

JOAN. *(Looking at the bottle.)* I can't believe we don't know what we're putting in our mouths. There oughta be a law.

DOTTIE. Well whatever it is, my family loves it.

(To **CONNIE.***)* But it's too spicy for the baby if you're…

(Gestures to her breasts.)

…feeding that way.

*(***CONNIE** *starts to cry.)*

Hormones.

CONNIE. Ugh. You may be right, Dottie.

(The timer goes off.)

JOAN. Come on Connie, help me! If we don't get these pretzels in at exactly the right time, this Jell-O is not gonna gel the way Jell-O should gel.

AGNES. What else do you think we should put in the Jell-O, Connie?

DOTTIE. Carrots?

JOAN. Cream cheese?

AGNES. Cucumber?

CONNIE. *(Smiling through tears.)* Coconut?

DOTTIE. And of course Reddi-wip on top. Whipped cream fixes everything!

*(***DOTTIE** *throws back her head and squirts the whipped cream into her mouth. Then squirts some into* **CONNIE***'s mouth.)*

CONNIE. The Jell-O mold is ready to go in the fridge.

AGNES. *(To* **CONNIE.***)* Here. This'll do the trick to calm you down.

*(***AGNES** *pours a nip of liquor into its bottle cap for* **CONNIE.** *The timer dings.)*

DOTTIE. Dr. Spock says that every pregnant woman must have two cocktails a day to "calm the nerves."

JOAN. And a cup of strong coffee at four o'clock so you can perk up and make dinner for your husband.

CONNIE. Ick. This tastes like toothpaste.

AGNES. It's crème de menthe.

> (**JOAN** *takes out some crystal champagne flutes.*)

DOTTIE. These glasses are gorgeous!

JOAN. Thank you. They're from Poland.

DOTTIE. How'd they get all the way over here?

JOAN. My Grammy Rose brought them here before World War II.

> (*Ding! They freeze. Lights change.*)

[MUSIC NO. 06A "DURING THE WAR"]

(*To audience.*) During the war, in America, women were taken out of the kitchen to work all the jobs vacated by the men who were off fighting. We were driving trucks, building ships, making bullets in factories. When the war was over, they marched us back to the kitchen, handed us a spatula and apron and said, "Thank you for your service."

> (*Lights back up. The others unfreeze.*)

CONNIE. What's that awful smell?

JOAN. (*Smells.*) The pu-pus!!

AGNES. I turned the oven up to five hundred, so they'd cook faster.

> (**JOAN** *runs for the oven.*)

DOTTIE. This is a disaster.

JOAN. Relax. They're fine. Caught in the nick of time.

DOTTIE. Agnes, you almost ruined everything. You never cook. You sit around, read magazines and paint your nails.

AGNES. You're right. I've finished everything I need to do! The food is cooking. So...it's happy hour!

[MUSIC NO. 07 "HAPPY HOUR"]

DOTTIE. Happy hour is five o'clock. It's only four o'clock.

JOAN. It's five o'clock in New York!

AGNES. Great! So, I'll make a Manhattan!

CONNIE. That's a man's drink.

AGNES. I'll put an umbrella in it.

DOTTIE. If we start drinking now, we'll never get our entry postmarked by five o'clock. And I've got my heart set on that second prize: a weekend at the Fontainebleau Hotel.

> (**CONNIE** *puts the cake in the oven.*)

AGNES. Well, the contest does say to create "a colorful cocktail." Just following the rules. Miami here we come!

> (**AGNES** *rolls out Joan's double-decker liquor cart. Grabs a bottle of rum.*)

> IT'S HAPPY HOUR
> HOW 'BOUT A MAI TAI OR A WHISKEY SOUR?

CONNIE.
> THEY SAY IT CALMS THE NERVES
> AT LEAST THAT'S WHAT I'VE HEARD

DOTTIE.
> PERFECT WITH POLYNESIAN PU-PU HORS D'OEUVRES

JOAN.
> WITH STRUGGLES DAY IN AND DAY OUT
> IT'S OUR OASIS IN A DROUGHT

DOTTIE. (*Referring to her drink.*)
> A BIG SLICE OF PARADISE

AGNES.
> YEAH, WHO COULD BEAT THE PRICE?

CONNIE.
> AND HOW!

ALL.
> IT'S HAPPY HOUR NOW!

DOTTIE.
> NOW IF I HAVE TO WIPE ONE MORE RUNNY NOSE
> IF I HAVE TO WASH ONE MORE LOAD OF CLOTHES

    I LOVE IT DON'T GET ME WRONG
    JUST GIVE ME SOMETHING STRONG

ALL.

    C'EST BON! IT'S HAPPY HOUR NOW!
    OOO-LA-LA-LA

DOTTIE & CONNIE.

    A LITTLE BREAK FROM

ALL.

    OOO-LA-LA-LA

DOTTIE & CONNIE.

    THE DAILY HUMDRUM

ALL.

    OOO-LA-LA-LA

> *(The phone rings.* **JOAN** *picks it up. By now they are tipsy.)*

JOAN. Hello?

DOTTIE. Don't tell me that's for me.

JOAN. Oh, hi. Let me see if she's here!

> **(DOTTIE** *waves her hands "no," but* **JOAN** *hands her the phone anyway.)*

DOTTIE. Mom!

> *(Listens.)*

Which one of the twins? Rub some Paregoric on his teeth.

> *(Beat.)*

I know he's not teething, but it'll put him out. As a matter of fact, put some on – the other twin too.

> *(Beat.)*

Mother, stop screaming! A turtle down the toilet isn't the end of the world.

> *(Beat.)*

Okay, yeah, for the turtle it is.

(**JOAN** *grabs the egg timer, winds it up, holds it up to the phone, and makes it go off.*)

DOTTIE. What? Ronnie? For heaven's sake. He's eight years old. He can take care of himself. Mom, Mom. I have total confidence that you'll get all three – I mean four – kids under control!

(To the others, with hand over mouthpiece.) For a second, I forgot how many I had. When you have that many that close together, it's all a blur.

(**DOTTIE** *back to the phone.*)

AGNES.

HERE I DON'T WORRY IF MY HEMLINE IS TOO SHORT

CONNIE.

HERE I GET DOSE OF SWEET MORAL SUPPORT

JOAN.

WHERE ELSE CAN WE GO THAT WOULD BE APROPOS?

DOTTIE.

ANYHOW,

DRINK UP, IT'S HAPPY HOUR NOW!

ALL.

A GRASSHOPPER WOULD BE NICE

A SIDECAR OR GIMLET ON ICE

A PLACE WE CAN DISAPPEAR

SECRETS ARE SAFE RIGHT HERE

CONNIE.

I'LL TOAST TO THAT!

AGNES. I wish there was a Dirty Mike's for women. A bar where a girl could go. Alone.

CONNIE. Without being thought of as a "lady of the night."

DOTTIE. We'll call it Filthy Fran's.

AGNES.

WHY CAN'T A GIRL SIT AT A BAR?

JOAN.

UNESCORTED, WITH A BIG CUBAN CIGAR?

AGNES. A "Crazy Cuban"!

DOTTIE. Where?

AGNES. That's our colorful cocktail! A "Crazy Cuban"! And we can use the juice from the can of pineapples and we've got the rum, and the banana liqueur!

ALL.

OOO-LA-LA-LA

JOAN & CONNIE.

A GREAT ESCAPE FROM

ALL.

OOO-LA-LA-LA

AGNES & DOTTIE.

THE DAILY HUMDRUM

ALL.

OOO-LA-LA-LA

JOAN.

IT'S HAPPY HOUR NOW!

ALL.

WE'RE PLOWED!

(*The doorbell rings.*)

DOTTIE. Who's that?

CONNIE. Fuller Brush Man?

AGNES. Avon calling?

DOTTIE. *Encyclopedia Britannica?*

[MUSIC NO. 07A "THE DOORBELL RINGS"]

(*Ding! They freeze.* **JOAN** *in spotlight.*)

JOAN. (*To the audience.*) Better. I read it when it first came out, but they were always sold out at the bookstore. And I was dying to see their faces when they read it. So I called my friend Cookie. She knew where to get everything. Cookie's the one who got me that vibrating hairbrush.

(Lights back up. The others unfreeze. **JOAN**
opens the front door. A hand is holding out a
book in a brown paper wrapping. **JOAN** *takes*
it, rips off the brown paper, and holds up the
book.)

JOAN. *The Kinsey Report on Human Female Sexuality*!

CONNIE. Joan, you didn't!

JOAN. Didn't I?

DOTTIE. I already have four kids. I don't wanna know how
to make more.

AGNES. Where's your handy pocket manual now, Dottie?

[MUSIC NO. 08 "SOMETHIN'S BURNIN'"]

CONNIE. Yeah. Move over, Joe Bonomo.

JOAN.

IT TOOK A ZOOLOGIST FROM INDIANA U.
IN A LAB WITH SIX THOUSAND VOLUNTEERS
TAKIN' ON A SUBJECT FORMERLY TABOO
CREATIN' SUCH A RUCKUS THE WORLD HASN'T SEEN IN
    YEARS

NEWS REPORTS, TV SHOWS
EVEN THE COVER OF *TIME* MAGAZINE
DECLARED AMERICAN SOCIETY WAS UNDER ATTACK
BUT I HEAR JUST READING IT OUT LOUD ACTS LIKE AN
    APHRODISIAC

ALL.

DOCTOR, DOCTOR, DOCTOR
ALFRED, ALFRED C. KINSEY
YOUR STATISTICS PROVE

JOAN.

THAT ODDLY ENOUGH THE HUMAN FEMALE

AGNES. *(Spoken.)*

THAT'S US GIRLS!

ALL.

LIKES IT TOO!
SOMETHIN'S BURNIN'

DOTTIE. *(Spoken.)*
    ARE YOU HOT?

ALL.
    SOMETHIN'S BURNIN'

DOTTIE. *(Spoken.)*
    IS IT ME?

ALL.
    OH MAN, IF HE CAN HIT THAT SPOT!
    READ ON, READ ON!

DOTTIE. No! I'm gonna go get the Jell-O.

    *(She goes to get it. And then briefly rethinks it
    and turns around for a second to come back
    to look at the book.)*

ALL.
    IN THE BACK OF THE ROOM OF THE LAB

DOTTIE. *(Reminding herself.)* No!

ALL.
    JUST IMAGINE ALL THE WHISPERS
    THE EVIDENCE WAS GATHERED AMID MOANS AND
        GROANS

JOAN.
    PIE CHARTS

CONNIE.
    DIAGRAMS

AGNES.
    PICTURES OF EROGENOUS ZONES!

JOAN.
    SIXTY-FOUR PERCENT OF ALL WOMEN HAD ONE

DOTTIE. *(Spoken.)*
    ONE WHAT?

JOAN.
    UNDER CERTAIN CONDITIONS

AGNES.
    I HEAR
    IT'S CLEAR
    THAT PERCENTAGE WENT UP SOME

JOAN.

ACTUALLY QUITE A BIT BY VARYING POSITIONS

CONNIE & DOTTIE.

OH!

ALL.

SOMETHIN'S BURNIN'

AGNES.

IT AIN'T THE FOOD

ALL.

SOMETHIN'S BURNIN'

CONNIE.

I'M IN THE MOOD

JOAN. *(To **DOTTIE.**)*

IF YOU CAN'T SAY IT, JUST SPELL IT

(Ding! A timer goes off.)

DOTTIE.

S...E...X?

JOAN, AGNES & CONNIE.

SEX!

DOTTIE.

SHH!

JOAN. My rump roast is ready!

CONNIE. It looks juicy.

DOTTIE. It sure does! Open the book!

(Beat.)

Close the book! Open the book! Turn the page.

JOAN. See anything you like?

CONNIE. Oh my gosh. I've never done that.

AGNES. I have. I think.

DOTTIE. It's upside down!

JOAN. No it's not.

AGNES.

HE'S TALKIN' 'BOUT
YOU 'N ME

JOAN.
AND THE GIRL NEXT DOOR
DOTTIE.
REALLY?
CONNIE. *(Spoken.)*
SYLVIA?
DOTTIE. *(Spoken.)*
PATRICE?
CONNIE. *(Spoken.)*
WANDA?
AGNES. *(Spoken.)*
LENORE?
DOTTIE. *(Spoken.)*
EVEN BETTY?
JOAN. *(Spoken.)*
BETTY.
CONNIE. *(Spoken.)*
CROCKER?
JOAN. *(Spoken.)*
CROCKER.
CONNIE, DOTTIE & AGNES. *(Spoken.)*
BETTY!

(Singing.)

TELL ME MORE!
ALL.
S-E-X
KEEP THE PAGES TURNIN'
S-E-X
'CAUSE SOMETHIN'S BURNIN'
S-E-X
LISTEN BOYS!
IT'S GONNA BE A
WHOLE
BRAVE
NEW
WORLD!

(**CONNIE** *bursts into tears.*)

JOAN. Connie, it's just a book about sex. It's not like we're reading *Gone with the Wind*.

DOTTIE. It's those darn hormones again.

(*To* **CONNIE**.) Here, have a purple pill.

AGNES. Don't cry, Connie. You're messing up your makeup.

CONNIE. (*Sobbing.*) Maybe it is the hormones. But I felt like this before I was pregnant.

DOTTIE. Why? Skip is everything you could want in a husband.

AGNES. He's wealthy.

JOAN. He's handsome.

(**CONNIE** *cries harder.*)

DOTTIE. And he's a wonderful figure skater.

CONNIE. (*Feeling a contraction.*) Uh-oh.

JOAN. What?

CONNIE. Uh-oh.

DOTTIE. She's going into labor! Call Skip!

[MUSIC NO. 09 "IN LIMBO"]

CONNIE. No! No!

DOTTIE. You need your husband by your side!

AGNES. Call JCPenney! Ask for Women's Shoes!

CONNIE. Don't call Skip!

(*To audience.*) Oh, how did this happen?

I CAN'T FORGET THE NIGHT WE MET, IT WAS ALL
    ARRANGED
THEY SAID WE'D MAKE THE PERFECT MATCH BUT
    SOMETHING ALWAYS FELT STRANGE
HE

ALL.

SLIPPED THE RING ON MY FINGER

CONNIE.

I THOUGHT THAT WOULD MAKE IT ALL RIGHT
THERE WAS SOMETHING

ALL.

    MISSIN' IN HIS KISSIN'

CONNIE.

    BUT THEY SAID I'D LOOK PRETTY IN WHITE

JOAN, DOTTIE & AGNES.

    UH-OH LIMBO

    UH-OH LIMBO

    UH-OH LIMBO

CONNIE.

    OH, I'M IN LIMBO

    WE HAD IT ALL FIGURED OUT,

ALL.

    THE HOUSE, THE MIMOSA TREE

CONNIE.

    HE AND ME AND BABY'D MAKE THREE

ALL.

    JUST LIKE A REAL FAMILY

CONNIE.

    WE

ALL.

    PUSHED THE TWIN BEDS TOGETHER

CONNIE.

    WE HAD A MONTHLY PLAN-NA

    BUT PRETTY SOON I NOTICED SOMETHING WAS VERY

        WRONG

ALL.

    WITH THE BANANA!

CONNIE.

    OH

JOAN, DOTTIE & AGNES.

    UH-OH LIMBO

    UH-OH LIMBO

    UH-OH LIMBO

CONNIE.

    OH, I'M IN LIMBO

    (To audience.) It was the only night Skip's bowling team

ever won. I think it was the new shirts I embroidered for them. "The Holy Rollers." The guys went to the bar to celebrate but I stayed behind because it was battle of the bands night at the Don Carter Lanes. I'd never heard anything like that band from Trinidad. There was something about that guy banging on those steel drums.

> SOMETIMES THE MUSIC MAKES YOU FEEL A HYPNOTIC HEAT

ALL.

> AAH!!

CONNIE.

> THE MOON WAS FULL, THE WINE SO SWEET HE SWEPT ME OFF MY FEET
>
> MY

ALL.

> HEART WAS BEATING OH SO LOUD

CONNIE.

> I COULD NOT HEAR MY HEAD SAY

ALL.

> "NO, STOP!"

CONNIE.

> NOW I'M COUNTING THE DAYS
> 'TIL THE BIG SURPRISE WHEN I

ALL.

> FIN'LLY POP!

CONNIE.

> DAY-O!

ALL.

> DAY-O! DAYLIGHT COME AND ME NO WANNA GO HOME

CONNIE.	**AGNES, JOAN & DOTTIE.**
UH-OH, OH I'M IN LIMBO	UH-OH, LIMBO
UH-OH, YA YA YA YA YA YO!	UH-OH, LIMBO
OH I'M IN LIMBO	UH-OH, LIMBO
UH-OH, DAY-O!	UH-OH LIMBO
BECAUSE OF HIMBO, I'M IN	UH-OH, LIMBO
LIMBO OH, OH, OH	UH-OH, LIMBO

UH-OH IN LIMBO, OH I'M   UH-OH, LIMBO
   IN
LIM–   UH-OH LIM–

  (**CONNIE**'s *water breaks.*)

DOTTIE. Connie, your water broke!

CONNIE. AAAHHH! What am I gonna do?

AGNES. Call Skip!

CONNIE. NO!

DOTTIE. Don't be silly! Give me the phone.

CONNIE. *(Doubled over with contractions.)* I said, don't call Skip!

AGNES. But he's your husband!

CONNIE. But he might not be the father of the baby!

  (Frozen panic and silence. Then:)

DOTTIE. She's not thinking clearly right now…when a woman goes into labor her mind just goes out the window!

JOAN. We gotta get her to the hospital.

CONNIE. *(To* **JOAN.***)* What have I done? Everyone's going to KNOW!

AGNES. I'll drive. I've only had three drinks. We can stop at the post office on the way.

CONNIE. *(To* **JOAN.***)* What am I going to say?

AGNES. *(To* **CONNIE.***)* Lie, Connie, lie! When the nurse hands you that baby, just cry, hold Skip's face lovingly and say, "It looks just like you, sweetie."

CONNIE. I can't. The baby…

DOTTIE. …Could be a little boy.

AGNES. …Could be a little girl.

CONNIE. …Could be a little black!

  (Beat. Shock.)

JOAN. I told you months ago, we won't know until you have the baby. And then we'll figure it out.

DOTTIE. *(To* **JOAN.***)* Joan, you knew?

JOAN. Yes. We should get to the hospital.

DOTTIE. *(To* **CONNIE.***)* Connie, you told her and not me?

CONNIE. *(To* **DOTTIE.***)* How could I tell you? You can't even look at a picture of Sidney Poitier. You're so prejudiced!

DOTTIE. We were going to be mothers together. I bought you a bassinet. You ruined everything.

AGNES. What about the contest?

> (**CONNIE** *is in full labor now.*)

CONNIE. OHHHH! FUCK THE CONTEST!

> *(They stop dead in their tracks.)*

JOAN. *(To* **CONNIE.***)* Calm down. Breathe.
> *(To* **AGNES.***)* Agnes, we're talking about Connie's life.

AGNES. This contest is my life.

> (**AGNES** *exits, carrying the envelope and the postcards.*)

DOTTIE. *(To* **AGNES.***)* Good. You have your contest.
> *(To* **CONNIE.***)* You have your baby.

JOAN. *(To* **DOTTIE.***)* Dottie, now's not the time. Don't be so narrow-minded and selfish.

> *(Ding! A timer goes off.* **DOTTIE** *goes to the oven and pulls the cake out.)*

CONNIE. Yeah, maybe there's a pill for that.

DOTTIE. Here. Here's your pineapple upside-down cake!

> (**DOTTIE** *turns the cake over and slams it on the counter.)*

I'm leaving!

> (**DOTTIE** *picks up her purse to leave and knocks over one of Joan's grandmother's champagne flutes.)*

JOAN. Grammy Rose's glasses!

> *(Joan's book falls to the floor.)*

> (**CONNIE** *has a major contraction. She starts to scream.)*

CONNIE. AAAAAAAAH!

> *(Ding!* **CONNIE** *freezes mid-scream, mouth open. Lights change.* **JOAN** *picks up her notebook and holds it up. Throws it in the trash.)*

JOAN. *(To audience.)* And that was the end of the Wednesday Winnetka Women's Cooking Club.

> *(***CONNIE** *unfreezes. Lights up.)*
>
> *(She continues the scream.)*

CONNIE. AAAAAAAAAAHHH!

[MUSIC NO. 09A "ACT ONE – PLAYOFF"]

> *(Musical stinger ends with a door slam on the final note. Curtain comes down as the sixties set changeover prepares for the reveal in Act Two.)*

ACT TWO

[MUSIC NO. 09B "ENTR'ACTE - INSTRUMENTAL"]

(Lights up. We are now in 1967. **JOAN** *comes out from behind the curtain. She is dressed in hippie-chic.)*

JOAN. Hello 1967! We went from Betty Crocker to Betty Friedan. Connie had a beautiful baby boy. Agnes ended up taking a Greyhound to New York. Dottie moved to the other end of town and I have my own syndicated daily column called "It's a Woman's World." Oh, and Ann-Margret lost to the Mexican leaf player. I tried to reach everyone in '60, Dottie hung up on me, no dice. Tried again in '63, Agnes was too busy. Connie told me to keep trying. And this time when I called a reunion of the Wednesday Winnetka Women's Cooking Club, BINGO! And boy have I got a big surprise!

[MUSIC NO. 10 "YA DIG?"]

IT'S HIGH TIME THAT WE ALL GET TOGETHER
BOP BOP BOO BEE DOO BOP!
(SPOKEN.) YA DIG?
THEY HAVE NO CLUE WHAT'S ABOUT TO HAPPEN
BOP BOP BOO BEE DOO BOP!
(SPOKEN.) IT'S BIG!
WAIT'LL YOU SEE MY BRAND-NEW KITCHEN!
YEAH, WAIT'LL YOU SEE MY PAD!
(SPOKEN.) IT'S BAD!
SOCK IT TO ME!

> *(**AGNES** enters from behind the curtain.)*

AGNES.
SOCK IT TO ME!

(**CONNIE** *enters from behind the curtain.*)

CONNIE.

SOCK IT TO ME!

(**DOTTIE** *enters from behind the curtain.*)

ALL.

YEAH YEAH!

AGNES.

I WONDER WHAT SHE LOOKS LIKE

ALL.

BOP BOP BOO BEE DOO BOP!

JOAN.

GROOVY!

CONNIE.

I CAN'T WAIT TO SEE HER

ALL.

BOP BOP BOO BEE DOO BOP!

JOAN.

OUTTA SIGHT!

DOTTIE.

SHE MUST BE UP TO SOMETHING

ALL.

BOP BOP BOO BEE DOO BOP!

JOAN.

FAR OUT!

AGNES.

I WONDER WHAT SHE

CONNIE.

WONDER WHAT SHE

DOTTIE.

WONDER WHAT SHE

AGNES, DOTTIE & CONNIE.

WANTS FROM ME?

ALL.

I SHOULDA TEASED MY HAIR
I SHOULDA SHORTENED MY SKIRT
I SHOULDA BROUGHT DESSERT

JOAN.

LAY IT ON ME

AGNES.

LAY IT ON ME

CONNIE.

LAY IT ON ME

DOTTIE.

LAY IT ON ME

(The curtain comes up, revealing Joan's sixties-chic remodeled home and an all-female band that has been playing the entire show. They are also dressed in sixties garb.)

ALL.

BOP BOP BOO BEE DOO BOP BOP BAH DOO DOO
BOP BOP BOO BEE DOO BOP!

CONNIE.

TAXI!

AGNES.

TAXI!

DOTTIE.

BUICK.

ALL.

BOP BOP BOO BEE DOO BOP BOP BAH DOO DOO
BOP BOP BOO BEE DOO BOP!

JOAN.

I HOPE THEY'RE NOT UPTIGHT.

WHOA

AGNES.

WHOA

CONNIE.

WHOA

DOTTIE.

WHOA

JOAN.

WHOA

AGNES.

WHOA

CONNIE.

WHOA

DOTTIE.

WHOA

ALL.

BOP BOP BOO BEE DOO BOP BOP BAH DOO DOO
BOP BOP BOO BEE DOO BOW!

JOAN.

COOL!

(The doorbell rings.)

[MUSIC NO. 10A "SIXTIES ENTRANCES"]

Come in!

*(**DOTTIE** walks in, wearing, in her own mind, a more fashion-forward dress. She is carrying a marble bundt cake.)*

Dottie!

DOTTIE. *(Matter-of-factly.)* I made your favorite cake.

*(She shoves the cake at **JOAN**. Freeze. Music stops.)*

JOAN. *(To audience.)* That's a good sign.

(Unfreeze. Music starts again.)

DOTTIE. And I can see your nipples.

JOAN. I burned my bra.

DOTTIE. You remodeled.

JOAN. Do you like it?

DOTTIE. When are the others getting here?

(The doorbell rings.)

*(**CONNIE** is clad in West Indian garb, sandals, and a colorful turban.)*

CONNIE. Hello?!

JOAN. *(To **CONNIE**.)* Connie Ballet-D'Lozieres from Trinidad!

CONNIE. *(In a French West Indian accent.)* You know it, girl. I took Andre's name.

(Sees **DOTTIE** *and drops the accent.)*

Hello Dottie.

*(***JOAN** *and* **DOTTIE** *exchange glances.)*

DOTTIE. A flight from Trinidad must have cost you a fortune.

JOAN. She owns her own travel agency.

CONNIE. *(West Indian accent.)* All I had to pay was the tax on the air fare!

DOTTIE. Out in the subdivisions, I might as well be coming from China.

CONNIE. You're still funny.

(Freeze. Music stops.)

JOAN. *(To audience.)* That's a good sign.

(Unfreeze. Music starts again.)

(The doorbell rings.)

*(***AGNES** *breezes in, sporting sunglasses, looking glamorous.)*

AGNES. *(To* **JOAN.***)* ¡Ay, que bonita! ¡El taxista no tenía cambio, y yo nada mas tenía billetes de cién, so le dí una propina grandisima!

[Oh, you look beautiful! The taxi driver didn't have change and all I had were hundreds, so I just gave him an enormous tip!]

(To all.) ¡Hola chicas! [Hello girls!]

JOAN & CONNIE. *(Excited.)* AGNES!

AGNES. *(Putting up her hand, she stops them dead in their tracks.)* Uh-Uh-Uh!

CONNIE & JOAN. Maria!

AGNES. Maria Magenta. *Mucho mejor.*

DOTTIE. *(Firmly.)* Okay, before we go any further. I need to clear up one thing.

(To **AGNES.***)* Why did Barbara try to steal Bo away from Nora when she knew Timmy had fallen down the well for five weeks and Vicky's house had burned down for the third time?

AGNES. Dottie, you watch my soap.

>   (*Freeze as* **AGNES** *kisses* **DOTTIE** *on the cheek.*)

JOAN. (*To audience.*) This is a good sign.

>   (*Unfreeze.*)

DOTTIE. Well, how else am I gonna get all my ironing done?

>   (*They all laugh.*)

> (*Looking closely at* **AGNES**' *face.*) You have Twiggy's eyelashes!

AGNES. It was the studio's idea.

>   (**AGNES** *pulls a beauty queen sash that reads "Miss TV Guide" out of her purse.*)

> I was voted Miss TV Guide last week! Did you see?

DOTTIE. No, I missed that.

AGNES. Page thirteen, bottom right-hand corner next to the crossword.

JOAN. Come on in everyone. Let's chill out in the den.

>   (*They move into the den and sit.*)

CONNIE. (*To* **AGNES**, *with the West Indian accent.*) And you look fantastique, girl!

AGNES. What's with the accent, Connie?

CONNIE. (*Drops her accent.*) What's with the accent, Agnes?

AGNES. (*Drops her accent.*) Okay, okay. We're in Winnetka.

CONNIE. You guys are a sight for sore eyes.

JOAN. Hands in!

>   (**JOAN** *puts her hand in. Then* **AGNES**, *then* **CONNIE**. *Finally* **DOTTIE**. *Team break.*)

ALL. Wednesday Winnetka Women! Woo!

CONNIE. Okay, Joan, you told us all to bring something. We're cooking?

AGNES. A celebration soup?

DOTTIE. Yeah, what are we celebrating?

CONNIE. (*Gasp to* **JOAN**.) You're pregnant.

DOTTIE. What?!

JOAN. No. You'll see. Now, who brought what?

CONNIE. I brought goat!

JOAN, AGNES & DOTTIE. Goat?!

>*(They look at* **CONNIE.***)*

CONNIE. Just kidding. I'm sick of goat. We have it five nights a week. I brought green bananas.

DOTTIE. Bananas in soup?

CONNIE. It's how chicken soup is made on the island.

DOTTIE. But won't the green bananas clash with my potato dumplings?

JOAN. You can make anything work. The most important ingredient in any recipe is the right amount of love from the hands that made it!

AGNES. *(To* **CONNIE** *and* **DOTTIE.***)* She's buttering us up for something.

JOAN. Don't be such a cynic, Agnes. What's in your bag?

AGNES. *Habanero* peppers and *vino blanco.* We drink the wine first so the soup tastes better.

[MUSIC NO. 11 "TEN YEARS"]

JOAN. Okay, pull out the cork and let's let it all hang out!

>*(No one talks.)*

Who's first?

ALL.
>I WONDER WHO WILL BREAK THE ICE?

CONNIE.
>NOT ME

AGNES.
>NOT ME

DOTTIE.
>NOT ME

JOAN.
>IT'S BEEN
>TEN YEARS

> LET'S PUT THE PAST TO BED
> TEN YEARS
> IT'S TIME TO MOVE AHEAD
> TEN YEARS
> LET'S SET ASIDE THE TEARS WE CRIED AND LET IT BE
>> *(No one volunteers.)*

Okay I'll start.

> WELL, BOB AND I ARE STILL TOGETHER
> YEAH, WE'RE STILL OKAY
> HE TAKES HIS BUSINESS TRIPS AND I WRITE EVERY DAY
> AND OVER THE YEARS I TOOK A TRIP OR TWO

DOTTIE.
> WHERE'D YOU GO?

JOAN.
> SAME OLD DOTTIE

AGNES.
> DOESN'T HAVE A CLUE

JOAN.
> COME ON GIRLS, ENOUGH ABOUT ME, NOW WHAT ABOUT YOU?

How's the family Dottie?

DOTTIE. I had another set of twins. Gary and Mary.

AGNES. More twins? How many do you need?

CONNIE. Can that happen?

JOAN. Obviously.

AGNES. That's why I have these babies.

> *(She reaches into her purse and brings out a familiar plastic container.)*

> FREE LOVE BABY
> THAT'S WHAT I SAY
> THESE DAYS EVERYONE KNOWS
> THAT ANYTHING GOES

DOTTIE. *(Horrified.)* Is that The Pill?

AGNES. Yep. You can get it on without getting pregnant.

JOAN. Right on!
> IT'S BEEN

JOAN & AGNES.

TEN YEARS

AGNES.

THE WORLD'S A DIFFERENT PLACE

JOAN & AGNES.

TEN YEARS

AGNES.

WE'VE BEEN TO OUTER SPACE

JOAN & AGNES.

TEN YEARS

IF MAN CAN TAKE A GIANT LEAP THEN SO CAN WE

AGNES.

COME ON CONNIE!

JOAN.

TELL US YOUR STORY!

AGNES.

WE'RE ALL TOGETHER NOW

JOAN & AGNES.

SING ON!

KEEP SINGIN' OUR SONG!

JOAN.

HOW'S SKIP?

CONNIE.

WELL SKIP LIVES IN WEST HOLLYWOOD, IT'S TRUE

JOAN.

THAT'S PERFECT!

AGNES.

I KNEW IT!

CONNIE.

AND I HAVE MY OWN BUSINESS NOW

WE'RE A HUGE SUCCESS!

JOAN & AGNES.

GOOD FOR YOU!

CONNIE.

COME ON DOTTIE.

IT'S BEEN

DOTTIE.

NO CALLS

CONNIE.

LET'S PUT THE PAST TO BED

DOTTIE.

NO MAIL

CONNIE.

IT'S TIME TO MOVE AHEAD

ALL.

TEN YEARS

CONNIE.

LET'S SET ASIDE THE TEARS WE CRIED AND LET IT BE

DOTTIE.

YOU CAN'T JUST SWEEP TEN YEARS UNDERNEATH THE
SHAG RUG.

JOAN. I know how hurt you were Dottie. We all were. We
were expressing our feelings. Just like all great women
do!

DIONNE AND TINA

CONNIE.

JONI AND JANIS

AGNES.

MAVIS AND ARETHA

JOAN, AGNES & CONNIE.

SING ON!

KEEP SINGIN' OUR SONG!

JOAN.

FORGET THE PAST

NO APOLOGIES

CAN WE LET BYGONES BE
BYGONES?

LET IT ALL GO, PLEASE?

THAT'S ENOUGH

	CONNIE, AGNES & DOTTIE.
ENOUGH ABOUT US	ENOUGH ABOUT, ENOUGH ABOUT US

DOTTIE.
> WHAT'S THE FUSS?
> NO MORE TO DISCUSS

JOAN.
> ALL I KNOW IS THAT IT'S SO GOOD TO SEE YOU
> ENOUGH ABOUT US!

ALL.
> LET'S DRINK A BIG TOAST TO WINNETKA WOMEN WOO!
> TEN YEARS!

JOAN. Remember girls? To your stations!

CONNIE. Just like old times.

DOTTIE. *(To* **AGNES.***)* If you had made it to the post office by five o'clock we might have won.

AGNES. Dottie, sixteen consolation prizes. We never had a chance.

JOAN. I still have the Betty Crocker corn holders.

DOTTIE. Well, I still dream about the Fontainebleau Hotel.

CONNIE. Joan, come on. Why are we really here today?

JOAN. Cool your jets. Hold your horses. Lay back. I'll tell you when I'm good and ready. More importantly, Connie, can't you move back to the states?

CONNIE. Well, we've thought about it, but with Andre and Andre Junior, we just fit in better there.

JOAN. Connie, come home! Biracial marriage isn't illegal anymore.

CONNIE. What's legal and what's accepted are two different things.

AGNES. Come live with me in Greenwich Village. Everything's legal there!

JOAN. Eartha Kitt is biracial and she's made history speaking out against Vietnam at a White House luncheon.

DOTTIE. *(Quietly.)* Ronnie's serving.

> *(Nobody really hears her.)*

AGNES. *(Responding to* **JOAN.***)* I heard about that! *(Imitating Eartha Kitt.)* "You send the best of this country off to be shot and maimed."

DOTTIE. *(Louder.)* I said my baby Ronnie is serving.

(There is another uncomfortable silence.)

JOAN. He's only eighteen.

DOTTIE. He's in Saigon. He enlisted.

JOAN. Don't worry, he'll be home soon. Right, girls?

CONNIE. Yes.

AGNES. Definitely.

DOTTIE. I'm so proud of him. He's serving his country just like his father did. He's not in Washington with those traitors burning their draft cards.

JOAN. The truth is no one should be over there. We're fighting an unwinnable war.

CONNIE. Besides, war is never a solution.

DOTTIE. You have no right to talk about this, Joan. You don't have kids.

AGNES. *(To **DOTTIE**.)* And you have enough for all of us!

*(**DOTTIE** stands up.)*

DOTTIE. I'm going.

AGNES. I'm sorry.

DOTTIE. I knew I shouldn't have come today.

JOAN. Dottie, we're sorry.

CONNIE. Yeah, we're sorry.

JOAN. Please stay. I didn't mean –

DOTTIE. Look, it's been a long time. Like you all said. Ten years. Things change. People change. And some people change more than others.

CONNIE. Dottie, don't be upset. Please sit down.

*(**DOTTIE**'s tears well up.)*

DOTTIE. Why? No one is listening to me anyway. Obviously, you all have done so much with your lives.

*(To **AGNES**.)* Famous.

*(To **JOAN**.)* Feminist.

*(To **CONNIE**.)* French.

JOAN. Dottie, please...

DOTTIE. You all have jobs. But nobody cares that I'm the president of the PTA. I raised thirty-three dollars and forty-two cents from the Winnetka Elementary bake sale to fix the playground seesaw! But you look at me and you probably think, "She's just a mom."

[MUSIC NO. 12 "JUST A MOM"]

I SWEAR I HAVEN'T SAT DOWN IN A YEAR
I FEEL LIKE A HAMSTER ON A WHEEL
I COULD FALL ASLEEP ON MY FEET RIGHT HERE
IT'S A FULL-TIME JOB JUST TO KEEP AN EVEN KEEL

I'm sorry I haven't had time to change the world. I've been busy changing diapers!

(*At tempo.*) SPIN CYCLES, RECITALS, BASEBALL, BALLET
YOU'RE ENJOYING THEATER, I'M AT THE SCHOOL PLAY
WHILE YOU'RE AT THE MOVIES I'M WATCHING CARTOONS
YOU'RE DANCING AT PARTIES, I'M BLOWIN' BALLOONS

KISSING BOO-BOOS
HOSING OFF MUD
SCRAPING OFF DOG DOO
SQUISHING SPIDERS IN THE TUB
BUBBLE BATHS
NEW MATH

I WAS JUST GETTIN' THE HANG OF THE OLD MATH!

MY IDEA OF A VACATION: GROCERY SHOPPING ALONE
HAVING TIME TO MYSELF: THE QUIET RIDE HOME
IF RUNNING OUT OF PATIENCE WAS AN EXERCISE
I'D BE IN GREAT SHAPE WITH BARBIE DOLL THIGHS

SLAYING DRAGONS BEHIND THE CLOSET DOOR
SINGING ALL THE NIGHTMARES AWAY
SCARY MONSTERS UNDER THE BED AND MORE
HOLDING MY BREATH WHEN THEY GO OUT TO PLAY

AS EVERYTHING SHIFTS AROUND ME
TELL ME HOW DO I FIT IN?
SO MANY NEW IDEAS SURROUND ME
TELL ME WHO AM I NOW? WHERE DO I BEGIN?

> WIPING TEARS
> CALMING FEARS
> CLEANING EARS AND THEN
> WAKING UP AND DOING IT ALL OVER AGAIN
> PATCHING PANTS, PINNING HEMS
> SEWING PATTERNS FOR THE PROM
> DON'T TELL ME
> IT NOT A JOB TO BE

JOAN. Dottie…

DOTTIE.

> JUST A MOM!
> JUST A MOM!

>> (**DOTTIE** *starts to storm out.*)

[MUSIC NO. 13 "THE WHOMP"]

JOAN.

> THAT REMINDS ME OF A COLUMN I WROTE
> ON THE NINTH OF SEPTEMBER
> THIS WOMAN SAID EXACTLY WHAT YOU SAID
> AND THAT MADE ME REMEMBER
> I DON'T KNOW THE WOMAN'S NAME
> BECAUSE SHE SIGNED HER LETTER
> "AT THE END OF MY ROPE IN SCHENECTADY"
> BUT IT WAS MY JOB TO FIND THE WORDS
> TO GIVE HER HOPE
> THAT'S WHAT SHE'D EXPECT FROM ME
> SO I ASKED HER:
> WHO PUT THE WHOMP
> IN THE WHOMP BOMPA LOO BOMP BOMP?
> IT'S A WOMAN!
> YEAH WHO PUT THE WHOMP
> IN THE WHOMP BOMPA LOO BOMP BOMP?
> YOU KNOW IT'S A WOMAN!
> IF YOU TRY TO DEFINE YOURSELF WITH JUST ONE NOUN
> REMEMBER, THERE'S A WHOLE LOTTA SHAKIN' GOING
>   DOWN
> 'CAUSE YOU PUT THE WHOMP IN THE WHOMP BOMPA
>   LOO BOMP BOMP

BECAUSE YOU'RE A WOMAN!

AGNES.

AND A WOMAN HAS ONE SIDE, TWO SIDES, THREE SIDES,
FOUR

FIVE SIDES, SIX SIDES, SEVEN, EVEN MORE

CONNIE.

SO DON'T DEFINE ME WITH JUST ONE NOUN

I'VE GOT A WHOLE LOTTA SHAKIN' GOIN' DOWN

JOAN.

BACK AWAY FROM THE DOOR, DOTTIE!

AND DO THE WHOMP!

DOTTIE.

NO!

JOAN.

WHOMP!

DOTTIE.

NO!

JOAN.

WHOMP BOMPA LOO CELEBRATE!

BECAUSE YOU'RE A WOMAN!

DO THE WHOMP!

CONNIE & AGNES.

WHOMP!

JOAN.

WHOMP!

CONNIE & AGNES.

WHOMP!

CONNIE, AGNES & JOAN.

WHOMP BOMPA LOO IT'S GREAT!

TO BE A WOMAN!

JOAN.

IF YOU THINK YOU'RE JUST A MOM

CONNIE.

OR A WIFE

AGNES.

OR A ROMP!

CONNIE, AGNES & JOAN.
> GET UP! ALL YOU GOTTA DO IS
> WHOMP WHOMP WHOMP!

JOAN.
> 'CAUSE YOU PUT THE

CONNIE, AGNES & JOAN.
> WHOMP

JOAN.
> IN THE

CONNIE, AGNES & JOAN.
> WHOMP BOMPA LOO BOMP BOMP!
> BECAUSE YOU'RE A WOMAN!

CONNIE. Today's Queen For A Day...

JOAN. With six children and a loving husband...

CONNIE. And CEO of the O'Farrell household...

AGNES. ...Let's hear it for her...

CONNIE, AGNES & JOAN. Mom of the Year!

> (**CONNIE** *takes flowers from a vase and hands them to* **DOTTIE** *as a bouquet. They drape* **DOTTIE** *in Agnes' "Miss TV Guide" sash and she becomes "Mom of the Year." With* **DOTTIE** *now on-board, they all celebrate together.*)

DOTTIE.
> I'LL DO THE WHOMP!

CONNIE, AGNES & JOAN.
> WHOMP!

DOTTIE.
> WHOMP!

CONNIE, AGNES & JOAN.
> WHOMP!

DOTTIE.
> WHOMP BOMPA LOO

ALL.
> CELEBRATE!

DOTTIE.
> BECAUSE I'M A WOMAN

I'LL DO THE WHOMP!

CONNIE, AGNES & JOAN.

WHOMP!

DOTTIE.

WHOMP!

CONNIE, AGNES & JOAN.

WHOMP!

ALL.

WHOMP BOMPA LOO IT'S GREAT
TO BE A WOMAN
IF YOU THINK YOU'RE JUST A MOM
OR A WIFE OR A ROMP

DOTTIE.

GET UP!

ALL.

ALL YOU GOTTA DO IS
WHOMP WHOMP WHOMP!

DOTTIE.

'CAUSE YOU PUT THE

CONNIE, AGNES & JOAN.

WHOMP

DOTTIE.

IN THE

ALL.

WHOMP

DOTTIE.

BOMPA LOO

ALL.

BOMP BOMP!
BECAUSE YOU'RE A WOMAN!
YEAH THIS WOMAN HAS ONE SIDE
TWO SIDES
THREE SIDES, FOUR
FIVE SIDES
SIX SIDES
SEVEN, EVEN MORE!
SO DON'T DEFINE ME WITH JUST ONE NOUN
I'VE GOT A WHOLE LOTTA SHAKIN' GOIN' DOWN

JOAN.
  GET DOWN!

DOTTIE.
  I'M A WOMAN!

CONNIE, AGNES & JOAN.
  TURN AROUND!

DOTTIE.
  I'M A WOMAN!

ALL.
  WHOMP WHOMP!
  I'M A WOMAN!

JOAN.
  YA BET YER BIPPY!

ALL.
  WHOMP!

> *(They are laughing, out of breath.)*

DOTTIE. Yeah, now you got it! I'm a mom and dammit, I'm a good one!

JOAN. Right on, sister!

CONNIE. Moms have the hardest job in the world.

AGNES. And you don't have a hair and makeup department to help you get ready.

DOTTIE. Ready? I'm always ready for anything. I'm a mom. Remember those pills? All those medicines for what the doctor called "hysteria." It was just another word for "motherhood." I threw every last pill in the trash.

> *(The others clap for her.)*

JOAN. *(Interrupts the clapping.)* Okay, if we're all coming clean…I'm not Joan Smith.

AGNES, DOTTIE & CONNIE. What?

JOAN. Real name…
  Chaia Bayla Frankel.

DOTTIE. You're Jewish?

CONNIE. But you love bacon.

JOAN. All Jews love bacon.

DOTTIE. I have a Jewish friend! I'm so happy!

AGNES. Is that why you called us here today? To tell us that?

JOAN. No, but I just wanted you to know. No reason to hide anymore. Not in this day and age.

CONNIE. And Bob knows you're Jewish?

JOAN. Connie, he's Jewish too.

DOTTIE. Two Jewish friends!

> (Beat.)

But you don't use your Jewish name in the paper.

JOAN. Does Pauline Esther Friedman use hers? No, she uses Abigail Van Buren.

AGNES. *(To JOAN.)* I read your column every day. I love Mondays – your "Women's Financial Independence" column.
And last week's when you wrote about the Equal Rights Amendment. Way to go!

DOTTIE. Jim reads it, too.

JOAN. He does?

DOTTIE. Uh-huh. He especially liked your "Tuesday Tips" column about lava lamps in the bedroom. Well, we both did.

JOAN. Did he see my column on vibrating pillows?

DOTTIE. Uh-huh.

JOAN. What about my piece on food and foreplay?

DOTTIE. I always said whipped cream fixes everything.

AGNES. *(To JOAN.)* You hot *tamale*.

JOAN. Grammy Rose would have wanted me to use Chaia Bayla Frankel, but I didn't want to deal with the mishegas.

AGNES. Okay, I have something to share, too. Here goes. You know Joe and Lucille were the best parents a girl could ever have. I didn't want to break their hearts so I never asked them about this. But I always knew I was different. Before I left for New York, I did a little digging and it led me to the St. Francis Orphanage.

CONNIE. You're adopted.

JOAN. Wow.

AGNES. There was no way I could really start fresh in New York until I found out where I came from. Who I really am. The nuns didn't have much information. They did give me a copy of my birth certificate. By the way, I'm a year younger. There it was on the birth certificate… "Race: Hispanic."

CONNIE. When the nurse handed me little Andre's paperwork, I got to the line that said "race" and I was proud for everyone to know the truth.

AGNES. That's exactly what the nun said to me: "You should be proud to know the truth.

[MUSIC NO. 14 "BLESSING IN DISGUISE"]

Your mother didn't make it while trying to leave Cuba to give you a better life."

I SPENT MY LIFE NOT KNOWING WHY
I STOOD OUT IN A CROWD
SHOULD I HANG MY HEAD IN SHAME?
SHOULD I NOT FEEL PROUD?
I FELT SO LOST AND ALL ALONE
THEN I FOUND MY WAY
AND LOOKING BACK IT ALL MAKES SENSE
IT LED ME TO TODAY

NOW LOOK AT ME
I CAN FLY HIGHER THAN THE STARS
I CAN DANCE CIRCLES 'ROUND THE MOON
I CAN DO ANYTHING I WANNA DO
'CAUSE NOW I SEE
IT WAS MEANT TO BE
WHAT MADE ME STAND OUT FROM ALL THE REST
MUCH TO MY SURPRISE
WAS A BLESSING IN DISGUISE

CONNIE.

EVEN WHEN I REACHED MY DREAM
AND PLAYED THE PART SO WELL
SOMEHOW I STILL FELT INCOMPLETE

BUT NO ONE ELSE COULD TELL
WHEN YOU'RE SURE THE TRUTH'S OUT THERE
YOU CAN'T IGNORE THE CALL
UNTIL YOU DIG DOWN DEEP INSIDE
YOU'LL NEVER HAVE IT ALL
NOW LOOK AT ME
I CAN FLY HIGHER THAN THE STARS
I CAN DANCE CIRCLES 'ROUND THE MOON
I CAN DO ANYTHING I WANNA DO
'CAUSE NOW I SEE
IT WAS MY DESTINY
WHAT MADE ME STAND OUT FROM ALL THE REST
I REALIZE
WAS A BLESSING IN DISGUISE
EV'RY SINGLE TEAR

AGNES.

EACH AND EV'RY HILL I HAD TO CLIMB

CONNIE & AGNES.

WAS THERE TO GET ME HERE
NOW LOOK AT ME
I CAN FLY HIGHER THAN THE STARS
I CAN DANCE CIRCLES 'ROUND THE MOON
I CAN DO ANYTHING I WANNA DO
NOW I SEE
INSIDE OF ME

CONNIE.

AND I CAN MAKE IT ON MY OWN

AGNES.

I KNOW I ALWAYS CAN COME HOME

CONNIE & AGNES.

IT'S CLEAR IT ALL HAS BEEN
A BLESSING IN DISGUISE

DOTTIE & JOAN.

BLESSING IN DISGUISE

DOTTIE. You both are so brave.

AGNES. This hair? This skin? This body? Come on girls,
don't tell me it didn't cross your mind.

DOTTIE. Well I did used to wonder how you always had a tan in the middle of winter. So that's how you can speak Spanish?

AGNES. No, silly! I took Spanish lessons.

CONNIE. Wow. You "passed" all these years here. That's why we raised Andre Junior in Trinidad. I didn't want him to try to "pass" in Winnetka.

JOAN. Connie, that's exactly why you need to come home. People are fighting for civil rights and you should be too. After all, Andre Junior is American.

CONNIE. I don't know, Joan. I'd be afraid for my little boy.

JOAN. Don't you get it? You're the New American Family. The melting pot. That soup we are making. That's it.

DOTTIE. I'll protect him. I'm the president of the PTA now. No one will mess with my Connie, or her child. Come back to Winnetka. You're not alone.

JOAN. We'll figure it out.

CONNIE. *(Beat, decides.)* I miss this. I want us to come home. I'm calling Andre!

> *(The others all react excitedly.)*

(To **JOAN**.*)* After six o'clock when rates are cheaper.

JOAN. Whoa. This is blowing my mind. I've got the perfect thing.

[MUSIC NO. 14A "ACAPULCO GOLD"]

> *(***JOAN*** takes a joint out.)*

MaryJane.

DOTTIE. Who's MaryJane?

CONNIE. Grass.

AGNES. Reefer.

JOAN. Acapulco Gold.

> *(***AGNES*** inhales. Freeze.)*

(To audience.) I had called them here to surprise them, and they surprised me. Leave it to my best friends. A bunch of smart, funny women talking about real issues. We weren't Gloria Steinem but we were the Wednesday

Winnetka Women and we had something to say. Our self-worth wasn't going to be measured anymore by the way we made a cup of coffee.

(Unfreeze. They are passing the joint around.)

AGNES. *(Exhales.)* I wish this shit was legal.

(She passes the joint to **CONNIE.***)*

I should do this more often.

CONNIE. *(Inhaling.)* Not as good as the ganja we get.

(She passes it to **DOTTIE.***)*

DOTTIE. Oh, NO! The police will smell it from outside! I have a Girl Scout meeting tonight. I don't have time to go to jail!

JOAN. Dottie, kick back. Just try it. It won't kill you and believe me, it will wear off by the time you see Jim. Besides, you only need one toke.

DOTTIE. *(Gives in.)* Oh, okay. I'm through fighting you all. You only live once, I guess. One toke. Here I go.

(She inhales and coughs. The others continue to pass the joint around.)

Am I supposed to feel something? I'm not feeling anything.

(Beat. Music stops.)

Do we have any Twinkies?

[MUSIC NO. 15 "FOOD"]

FOOD.

JOAN.

I'M TALKIN' FOOD.

CONNIE.

GOOD FOOD.

AGNES.

HOT FOOD.

DOTTIE.

FOOD. NOT CHEESE FONDUE

AGNES.

WE USED TO COOK

CONNIE.

NOT YOU

DOTTIE. *(Obviously feeling the effects of the pot, sings with a new passionate attitude.)*

JOAN, REMEMBER WHEN WE WERE COOKIN'
AND YOU BROUGHT THAT BOOK IN
AND WE WERE SHOCKED?
WELL, IT TURNED OUT THAT JIM KNEW ALL THOSE
     POSITIONS AND MORE
NOW OUR DOOR IS ALWAYS LOCKED
BECAUSE WE NEVER KNOW WHEN THE KIDS ARE GONNA
     BARGE IN
WHEN I'M ABOUT TO HAVE A BIG ONE,

> *(Now she has her eyes closed and is singing full out.)*

AND THERE MIGHT BE ONE MORE
TO COME
I NEED SOME

> *(She opens her eyes.)*

M&M'S
THE ONES WITH THE PEANUTS

> *(She sees the others are staring at her. She takes her time and then continues on.)*

OH YOU KNOW THAT I GET HUNGRY
AND I GET HUNGRY EV'RY NIGHT
OH YEAH YEAH YOU KNOW HOW I GET HUNGRY
I JUST GOTTA GRAB A BITE
YEAH DID I TELL YOU 'BOUT MY MAN?
AND HIS GREAT BIG APPETITE?

Tell us about Andre, Connie!

CONNIE.

HE LIKES HIS SUGAR IN THE MORNIN'
HE STIRS IT ALL AROUND AND AROUND AND AROUND
     AND AROUND AND AROUND AND AROUND

HE LIKES HIS HONEY IN THE EVENIN'
WHEN THE SUN IS GOIN' DOWN
FROM DUSK TO DAWN I KEEP MY MAN
THE SWEETEST MAN IN TOWN

> (**CONNIE** *takes a bite out of a banana and spits it out.*)

I forgot these are green bananas!

DOTTIE & CONNIE.

WHEN YA GOT IT GOOD
THEY'LL COME A-KNOCKIN' AT YOUR DOOR
YEAH WHEN YA GOT IT GOOD
FILL 'EM UP UNTIL THEY BEG FOR MORE

ALL.

AND MORE AND MORE

AGNES.

MARIA LIKES IT SPICY YEAH, YEAH
WITH HER HOT SAUCE ON THE SIDE
OOO MARIA LOVES IT SPICY
SHE LIKES HER BEANS REFRIED
SHE NEEDS THE WHOLE ENCHILADA
TO KEEP HER SATISFIED

JOAN. *(To the others.)* Gimme a food! Come on!

CONNIE. Jelly rolls!

DOTTIE. Pickles!

AGNES. Cherry pie!

JOAN. I can do that!

I BAKE HIM CHERRY PIE
YOU KNOW MY OVEN'S GOOD AND HOT
YES, I CAN SERVE THAT CHERRY PIE
I PUT THAT CHERRY RIGHT ON TOP
I LIKE IT ON TOP
AND WHEN HE FILLS ME WITH HIS KISHKE
THAT MAN CAN REALLY HIT THE SPOT

AGNES & JOAN.

WHEN YA GOT IT GOOD
THEY'LL COME A-KNOCKIN' AT YOUR DOOR

YEAH WHEN YA GOT IT GOOD
SERVE IT UP AND HELP YOURSELF TO MORE

ALL.

WHEN YA GOT IT GOOD
THEY'LL COME A-KNOCKIN' AT YOUR DOOR
YEAH WHEN YA GOT IT GOOD
FILL 'EM UP UNTIL THEY BEG FOR MORE
AND MORE AND MORE!

CONNIE. I'm hungry.

JOAN. Soup's almost ready! Last ingredient, girls – fresh tomatoes from my backyard! Now all we have to do is let it simmer.

> *(As she puts her tomatoes in the soup, she sees the Joe Bonomo book on the counter.)*

Oh girls, I saw this at the supermarket and saved it for you. Remember Joe Bonomo and his "handy pocket manuals for women"? ...This is the last one he wrote.

> *(She pulls out the little manual.)*

CONNIE. What's it called?

JOAN. *What I Know About Women.*

DOTTIE. What does he know?

JOAN. Here. Check it out for yourself.

DOTTIE. There's nothing in here.

JOAN. Exactly. Sixty-four BLANK pages! He finally admitted he knew nothing about women! And girls, hold on to your hats. Betty Crocker? Wasn't a real person. Didn't exist. Made-up.

DOTTIE. Betty Crocker doesn't exist.

CONNIE. So "Betty Crocker" was a crock of –

JOAN. – She was.

AGNES. Poor "Betty." The first woman to make a million dollars and never see a penny of it!

JOAN. Okay, everybody. I'm ready to tell you my big surprise.

> *(**JOAN** pulls out her old notebook.)*

Dig this. I'm gonna be published. I'm an author. At least the right people in New York, New York think so. Pull up a chair, ladies, I'd like to introduce you to *A TASTE OF THINGS TO COME*.

CONNIE. What's it about?

JOAN. It's a book. About us. Our cooking club.

AGNES. Well I'll be damned. You were always writing while we were cooking. Is this what you were up to all along?

JOAN. I told my publisher that we couldn't go to print without asking your permission. And of course, you'll all share in the royalties.

AGNES. I want my contract to explicitly say that I play myself in the movie version.

CONNIE. So you WERE buttering us up. I don't know about this. I have my family to think about.

DOTTIE. Joan, you always told us that what we said in the kitchen was private.

JOAN. Dottie, you were right before. Things change. People change.

DOTTIE. But my feelings were personal. That was between us. I never thought you'd share our secrets with anyone.

JOAN. *(To* **DOTTIE** *and* **CONNIE**.*)* What are you so afraid of? Our stories could give other women the courage to be who they want to be. Listen to my preface.

[MUSIC NO. 16 "IN TIME"]

(Reads from her book.) "There was a time in my life when I lived for one precious day a week. A day with the girls. It was the only time we could be free. All that time spent in tight buns and stiff girdles, we would finally let our hair down and breathe. We were in the kitchen along with millions of other women, changing the world. In hindsight, those hours, once a week with my best friends Dottie, Connie, and Agnes, are what made me who I am today."

WAS IT A MILLION YEARS AGO?

'CAUSE IT FEELS LIKE YESTERDAY

RIGHT HERE MAKING MEMORIES
AT OUR OWN LITTLE SOIRÉE
WE THUMBED THROUGH SCENES IN MAGAZINES
IMAGINED WHO WE'D BE
WE PUT OUR DREAMS ON LAYAWAY
FOR THE DAY THAT WE'D BREAK FREE

JOAN, AGNES & CONNIE.
IN TIME

JOAN.
WE STOOD THE TEST OF

JOAN, AGNES & CONNIE.
TIME

CONNIE.	**JOAN & AGNES.**
I GUESS WE STOOD THE TEST OF	IN TIME

JOAN, AGNES & CONNIE.
TIME

JOAN.
WASN'T IT A WONDERFUL WORLD
EVERY WEDNESDAY AFTERNOON?

AGNES.
WEDNESDAY AFTERNOON

JOAN & CONNIE.
BLENDING THE BITTER AND THE SWEET

AGNES.
IT WAS OVER MUCH TOO SOON

DOTTIE.
ALL THE BITS AND PIECES
DOWN TO EVERY LITTLE CRUMB

JOAN.
WAS FOOD FOR THOUGHT IN RETROSPECT
AND A TASTE OF THINGS TO COME

JOAN, AGNES & CONNIE.
IN TIME

DOTTIE.
HOW COULD WE KNOW WHO WE'D BE IN

AGNES, CONNIE & DOTTIE.

TIME

JOAN.

SOMETIMES THINGS TAKE TIME

JOAN, AGNES & DOTTIE.

IN TIME

CONNIE.

HOW COULD WE KNOW WHO WE'D BE IN

JOAN, CONNIE & DOTTIE.

TIME

AGNES.

SOMETIMES THINGS TAKE TIME

DOTTIE.

SECRETS JUST BETWEEN US

WE SWORE OUR LIPS WERE SEALED

CONNIE.

LITTLE DID WE KNOW BACK THEN

THAT ALL WOULD BE REVEALED

JOAN, AGNES & CONNIE.

IN TIME

DOTTIE.

SO MUCH LEFT TO DO

AGNES, CONNIE & DOTTIE.

IN TIME

JOAN.

SOMETIMES THINGS TAKE TIME

JOAN, AGNES & DOTTIE.

IN TIME

CONNIE.

SO MUCH LEFT TO DO

JOAN, CONNIE & DOTTIE.

IN TIME

AGNES.

SOMETIMES THINGS TAKE TIME

JOAN. Chapter One: JOAN – "To be successful in cooking, as in life, you have to find that delicate balance."

AGNES. Chapter Two: AGNES – "Take chances and add a little zest even if the recipe doesn't call for it."

CONNIE. Chapter Three: CONNIE – "Once in a while, it's good to stir things up a little."

DOTTIE. Chapter Four: DOTTIE – "Whipped cream fixes everything."

JOAN.

> IT'S NOW OR NEVER
> TAKE A LEAP IF YOU DARE
> TRUST YOUR HEART
> IT'S A START
> YOU'LL LAND SAFELY SOMEWHERE
> IN TIME

Don't you see, girls? We didn't come this far to not go farther. We need to move ahead, together, unafraid.

> *(It sinks in.)*

CONNIE. Let's do it!

AGNES. I can see my first close-up.

DOTTIE. I'm in. But you'll never get me to burn my bra.

> *(A timer goes off.)*

CONNIE. Soup's ready! Let's celebrate!

DOTTIE. *(Pronouncing it incorrectly.)* L'Chai-am!

JOAN. Here's to *A TASTE OF THINGS TO COME*!

CONNIE. And to being anything we want to be!

AGNES. Yeah! Anything!

JOAN. Author.

CONNIE. Astronaut!

DOTTIE. Maybe even President.

ALL.

> NO MATTER HOW MUCH YOU THINK YOU KNOW
> LIFE CAN BE SO STRANGE
> AND AS THE YEARS GO BY YOU SEE
> HOW MUCH THE TRUTH CAN CHANGE

JOAN, AGNES & DOTTIE.

> IN TIME

CONNIE.

I GUESS WE STOOD THE TEST OF

AGNES.

SOMETIMES THINGS TAKE

CONNIE & AGNES.

TIME

JOAN & DOTTIE.

HOW COULD WE KNOW WHO WE'D BE

JOAN, AGNES & DOTTIE.

IN TIME

CONNIE.

SO MUCH LEFT TO DO IN

AGNES.

SOMETIMES THINGS TAKE

CONNIE & AGNES.

TIME

JOAN & DOTTIE.

HOW COULD WE KNOW WHO

ALL.

WE'D BE IN TIME

(Curtain comes down slowly on the last few bars of music.)

(Curtain and lights up for bows.)

[MUSIC NO. 17 "BOWS / THE WHOMP – REPRISE"]

ALL.

DO THE WHOMP!
WHOMP!
WHOMP BOMPA LOO CELEBRATE!
BECAUSE YOU'RE A WOMAN!
I'LL DO THE WHOMP!
WHOMP!
WHOMP BOMPA LOO IT'S GREAT!
TO BE A WOMAN!
IF YOU THINK YOU'RE JUST A MOM
OR A WIFE

OR A ROMP!
GET UP! ALL YOU GOTTA DO IS
WHOMP WHOMP WHOMP!

'CAUSE YOU PUT THE
WHOMP
IN THE WHOMP BOMPA LOO BOMP BOMP!
BECAUSE YOU'RE A WOMAN!

(Actors exit as a reprise of "Cookin'" is heard.)

The End